I0616466

True Stories
and
Rhymes
of the
Range

George Fischer
The Last DK Cowboy

Copyright

© Copyright 2015, 2017 by George Fischer.
All rights reserved.

No part of this book may be reproduced, stored in a retrieval system, or transmitted by any means, electronic, mechanical, photocopying, recording, or otherwise, without written permission from the author.

ISBN: 978-1-941345-58-0

NOTE: *All events described in this autobiographical work were shared through the perceptions of the author. Some people depicted may not be identified by their real name.*

Table of Contents

INTRODUCTION:

I have written these stories about time spent a-horseback over half a century. Long, long ago while riding and camping during employment mostly at the DK RANCH. On this vast, over 200 section, Arizona cattle and horse operation many days were spent alone at various cow-camps. I say, alone, but not really. I was accompanied by many good cow-horses and some very ambitious cow-dogs. I never felt alone with these faithful, dependable pards.

RANCHERO

AUTHOR George Fischer

We drank the purest of water in the world from cold mountain wells, springs and captured rain. I admit my Arizona has now become too over populated for this cowhand. I don't like the changes. Arizona was just fine the way I found it, February of 1949.

Too bad so many folks have learned about Arizona... But, after all, they didn't stop me from showing up and staying. There was, however, one very big difference. I never did, or ever wanted to... *change* anything!

Days out in that rugged wild country were excitingly spent doing all that cowboys do. Packing equipment, feed and salt to livestock plus all the game who needed it, too. Giving attention and care to a thousand head of cattle. Repairing hundreds of miles of fence, cleaning and improving springs and riding, riding, riding most of the time

Sometimes I used a hand-axe to blaze trails over the high mountainous upper half of the ranch's sections. Always astride strong, willing, but sometimes fractious cow ponies. Forever searching for, tracking and herding cattle.

Trail time was spent renewing those old blazes, from a-horseback, along the best trails. Repairing these cliffside paths was an annual necessity. Time past happily, as I removed fallen trees, rocks and large boulders. Using my horse, ropes, hands and muscles was the only way! All this became very helpful when I returned in the late fall and winters.

Then, to trail up the remnant cattle and stray bulls that seemed to become individual hermits that time of year. The blazes helped me to find and travel the snow covered trails. Some bulls acted like they could spend the entire winter down in Sycamore Canyon at Kelsey Spring, Babes Hole and Winter Cabin. Well sure 'nuff, I'd finally track them down... usually in bunches of one! Zane Grey described this Sycamore Canyon vividly when he wrote his novel, *Thirty Thousand On The Hoof.*

Alone in this vast wilderness, I branded, cut and ear marked late summer calves. Other days I sometimes milked out angry horned mother cows that had one or two enlarged teats which their new calf hadn't been able to sufficiently nurse at. Rough work done by myself while loving every bit of it. Always using extreme caution so not to get myself injured beyond repair, or help.

Staying in remote, run-down log cabins that had both the enduring charms and the hazards of a wilderness. Sleeping among rats, mice, rattlesnakes, daddy long-legged spiders and other varmints. Winter Cabin permanently had a resident skunk. To shoot or evict him in any way meant living for days with the strong odor he'd produce if annoyed in the least. As our time together past, we had an agreement. He would only use the back, slightly ajar, door of this lengthy cabin and I would enter in and exit out of the front door.

My area contained cupboards, wood fired cook stove and wood heating stove. Also a table, two sleeping cots and feed bin. The skunks cozy area had the hay storage. Hay we packed in a-horseback thru out the summer for our fall and winter visits. For many years, at different times, this skunk and I had a pleasant, safe, mutual compromise.

Living almost silently gave me rewarding sights. Once I spotted an albino deer. A doe all so beautifully white. Years ago, lightly hunted deer lived to be very old. Buck racks were covered with points too numerous to count when a deer was bounding away. One old buck we saw regularly, near Sycamore Pass, we named "HatRack." With maybe ten points to a side, he was a magnificent sight to encounter.

CHAPTER ONE

A Prophet with Antlers

This true story took place in 1956 Arizona. It deals with a rancher and cowboy dilemma then and now. There is no solution to this problem, but this antlered friend of mine had his own ideas about escaping life's intrusions.

You may need lots of grey in your whiskers to understand this authentic tale. It originated long ago when Arizona was still young and wild. Only a State then for a short spell. Many cowpunchers still wore six-shooters and carried a Winchester rifle in a saddle scabbard. Game was plentiful and many even died from old age instead of an old hunter. Wild creatures had never encountered a human yet. Especially those critters living in the depths of Sycamore Canyon west of Sedona, Arizona.

Magnificently antlered buck deer grew up healthy and large while climbing those rough jagged slopes to graze. Their only enemy, the stealthy cougar, made them alert and quick to escape at the slightest sound of a surprise encounter. Their multi-pointed racks were impossible to count when they were bounding off on the run. Still cowboys tried to count them because each point on one side revealed their years on this earth. They usually were gone from view by the time we counted seven or so. Old Hatrack we named one buck carrying so many points, jumbled around on his noble head, that we never made a proper tally. Still... we always tried to be the one to get that number correct! They were interwoven and tangled which sometimes caused death for two bucks. Struggling to their death while in playful or serious battle that they could never untwine from.

Deep in that canyon one day, but still not on the actual floor of the chasm, I was making a casual ride checking on our supply of salt-lick and our cattle's general welfare. My briskly striding horse was picking his own way down a long narrowing ridge to the area of Barney Mesa. Barney Spring was still far below us as I entered into the holding area we built using the topography of this mesa to create a pasture.

Sycamore Canyon was so deep that even partly down into it you would still find high mesas before reaching the bottom. This mesa's top was shaped like a horseshoe. Encircled by nearly one hundred foot high cliffs, that required no fencing to hold livestock. We only fenced a mere fifty yards, cliff to cliff, between the heels of the horseshoe and added a gate. The result, a 100 acres of holding pen full of grass. Barney Mesa's topography made it easy for us to build this pasture because we, thankfully, packed in a lot less fencing materials on our horses, from the rim top seven miles above.

The only other exit was at the center toe of the horseshoe. A quarter mile narrow trail *straight down* to Barney Spring. One of the few trails that made some 'punchers lead their horse both up and down. I usually rode a circle and planned ahead to only traveled downhill on this trail. I sure didn't cherish making that winding, steep, *uphill* struggle too often.

Cattle and game that are left to their own life never hurry. They traveled up and down perilous trails, to and from water, smoothly and carefully. Taking all the time they needed to navigate tricky places to satisfy their thirst. Your horse, being of an impatient nature, must be taught to travel like they do... "When roaming do as the roamers do!"

At the far edge center it was easy to close off this precarious downhill trail to the spring. The boulder strewn steep edge squeezed in to just a doorway like trailhead. A doorway where we could block the trail by using five or six large thick dead cedar tree limbs. Thereby stopping passage to and from the mesa.

Below at Barney Spring we all admired and enjoyed the two hewn out, long, connected Ponderosa logs that captured fresh water for cattle and game. That constant overflow of spring water created a seasonal downhill garden of precious grass and other beneficial growth. That afternoon the mesa seemed empty as I headed for that rock strewn path down to Barney Springs. About half way in I spotted off to my left Old Hatrack. I had surprised him and he bounded off further to the left. This put me blocking his return path, both down to the spring and back out to the fenced entrance. Of course he could jump the fence anywhere he got to it but I rode back and forth, without crowding him, to keep him from coming in my direction. He was most comfortable when forty yards away from me and my horse. To him we were just another, but unusual, four legged beast.

Some places the manzanita, juniper, cedar and oak brush was very thick. I used these natural obstacles to help herd the big old Buck away from us and the gated fence behind me. Also slowly, zig-zagging back and forth so he could not break for the rocky downhill exit to the spring trail. The thick brush still kept me from getting a good count on his numerous points. I was staying too far away for a good look at him. This was my best shot at getting a perfect count. Still, if I crowded him too much, he could dash madly anywhere, even right over us to pass.

It was as if making cautious moves on a chessboard and you know how long chess games go on. We handled our wild cattle in this same manner. Slowly getting them accustomed to our presence while pointing them in the right direction. It was a beautiful afternoon for this pleasant, friendly game. Nothing was too desperate...Yet! The cliff's edge was getting closer and we both were becoming aware of that. Old Hatrack began to show his anxiety by making more hurried escape dashes to the left and right. This caused me to lose count, over and over, of his more than eighteen points. Even at that he was over nine years old. I paused now at this moment in the game, sensing the distress I had caused him by intruding on his usually serene existence. *Yes, animal faces do have expressions.*

At that moment I strangely realized this scenario was also taking place in my own life. Civilization was changing the way I, too, moved about in this overcrowded, populated Arizona. Pushing at me, my friends and families from all sides. Our horizons, once a beautifully calm, quiet, smogless world, were becoming overcome by an invasion of unpleasant interactions. Neither he nor I had any choice or refuge to escape to. His usually big soft eyes now became an excited, powerfully intense stare...Then he wheeled around and without hesitation, gracefully leaped off that high bluff into his uncluttered life.

I was shocked and amazed. My jaw dropped in breathless surprise. I loped over to the edge of the precipice with dreaded apprehension, frantically looking down. Over eighty feet below us were huge masses of overgrown, impenetrable oak brush. Deep in there, struggling on his back, then bounding upright, appeared Old Hatrack. Seemingly his old self in his own familiar surroundings. He shrugged off the sticks and leaves from his hide. Then easily handled leaping and weaving away thru the thick brush to parts unknown. I watched as he became lost in the wooded distance. Gratefully thanking our God for Hatrack's salvation.

Now when this dangerous, damaged, congested, confusing world swirls around me relentlessly, I recall that encounter. Old courageous Hatrack taught me, importantly, there will always be an escape route if you dare to take it.... Will I?... Will you?

CHAPTER TWO

Arizona

My early years of Arizona cowboyin' I worked at almost every ranch in the Verde Valley of central Arizona. Hiring out to any ranch I could as a typical roving, vagabond cowpoke. Often I came upon large herds of antelope at the Bull Pen Ranch outside of Camp Verde. I was riding for Irvin Walker at the M Diamond Ranch then. One interesting morning a nearby antelope herd became startled when I rode up. They stampeded from my horseback approach, wildly running downhill. As they turned far below me, leaping over a barbed-wire fence, I began to count the ripple they made clearing over the fence in twos and threes at a time. By steadily sighting down my finger to count the top of that ripple I reckoned there were over 300 antelope. Now they roam in small families and avoid the large meadows sometimes ringed with telescopic sights...

During those years bull elk grew to weigh over 1,000 pounds. A far cry from today's bull elk. Turkeys were always in flocks of 50 or more. Porcupines, raccoons, chipmunks, jack rabbits and little cottontails were my daily entertainment on a lonesome ride. Bears, both black and brown, also surprised us when we rode the high altitude trails above 4,500 feet.

Sometimes fleeing in rapid bursts of speed. On other chance encounters they lazily viewed us as they ate from their chosen berry bushes. Only to leave slowly when we approached for a better look.

Not so numerous were encounters with mountain lions. The stealthy cougar avoided man at all times. Only a fleeting sighting when our trails accidentally crossed. Without hunting dogs, I was fortunate to see cougars just a mere 5 times in over fifty years of riding in their wild habitat.

Wildlife are always such an enjoyable part of cowboys life. I had much admiration for the many different species and their mannerisms. They could be soft and friendly, or bared teeth ferocious all in the space of a minute. Frightened or curious, depending on how you approach them. The impressions I always treasure were how beautiful are each and every one of them... Especially their little off springs.

I'm now ashamed to say, I caught and kept for pets, many of those little critters. Just for a week, sometimes longer, for companionship, care, and play. Then I'd return them to the safety of their world when they were old enough. All those years I never carried a camera. I'm blessed that their appearances are still engraved, in color, on my memory. With a camera I could have also shown you parts of all these stories. We could have seen, together, the marvelous, fantastically beautiful life I was privileged to experience.

I only carried a rifle, a pistol and a lariat. Sometimes jerky, a can of fruit, medicine, wire pliers, and some repair wire. Also, behind my saddle was tied a worn yellow slicker for the very infrequent, but deluging rains. Never used a canteen that would annoyingly and continually bounce around on my knee. I could find a drink anywhere, or wait for a brief rainstorm to leave puddles on a rock. When desperate I drank from any muddy water hole that must always have live bugs in it. Just fan the bugs away and drink from what lies below the immediate surface. Never to drink from a bug-less puddle. Swallows from those could make you sick or even cause death.

Now, I wish I had carried that camera. In place of that often missed photo opportunity I still had a poetic mind to instill the same illustrious rhyming picture results. Here, together, let us reminisce among those fond memories. I hope these stories and poems paint a memorable, portrait like picture, for you too.

Bless God's World and we who use it... Sadly, beyond its limits...

Leaving New York for Arizona, to be a real cowboy, I have much to recount about my approach, adjustment, and surprises. These stories begin in 1949 with my initial impressions, meeting lasting new friends, who helped keep me on that cowboy trail. It goes on to follow almost sixty years of cowboyin' and ranching. Including many adventures while riding bronco horses in the deep wild canyons of central Arizona. True accounts of wild animals, wild cattle, rough horses, and fearless men who rode that territory.

For exciting picturesque scenes, sprinkled with chuckles, surprises and true adventures... read on...

CHAPTER THREE

1949

Author on Cherry

This first Arizona employment I found in an outdoor magazine ad. They responded to me after numerous mailing attempts to gain a cowhand ranch job from advertised sources, including the railroads that shipped cattle. This particular 1949 employment turned out to be clearly very western, but not the cowpuncher job I had envisioned, dreamed and wished for during seventeen years of New York existence.

I arrived after four days and four nights of torturous travel on a Continental bus. Seemed like that dang bus stopped at every town along the way. I learned to stay on the bus late evenings until people exited the long last seat across the rear. Capturing that seat gave plenty of sleeping space and leg room for the long night miles. It was the big winter of 1948-49. I was seventeen with only twelve dollars left of cross country expenses. All possessions stuffed in a small black suitcase held shut with a worn leather belt.

CHAPTER FOUR

The Train Depot

PRE-SPRING SNOWFALL

Flagstaff, Arizona had seven foot of snow, with fourteen foot drifts. Most of the trip was on Route 66 until Flagstaff. Arriving at 2:00 A. M, on a well below zero February night, I wished for a warmer jacket as the bus roared away, continuing on west to a warmer California. Now there were hours to wait for the next bus south down highway 89A to Cottonwood. I still can envision that dark Railroad Depot that also served as the only bus terminal. This old building was destined to be my jumping off place to a new lifetime.

It was not invitingly warm or pleasant that night. Only one attendant handed out a bus schedule with a brief nod. He soon returned to his napping. Long wooden benches close to a large pot-bellied wood stove needing more wood, seemed to invite sleep. I planned to stretch out there for a little while before daylight. I soon dozed off.

Sometime later, a cold blast from an opening door awakened me. The three silhouetted figures at the doorway, wearing western hats, looked to me like cowboys! I pretended sleep as they stumbled past me. They were not cowboys, but Indians! I did not then know the term "Native Americans". I found out later, the cowboys just called them all by the name, "Chief." They did not sport any feathers, however and except for their Navajo language, they sure did look like cowboys to me with their Levi Jackets and trousers. It was obvious they had hoisted plenty of "fire-water" that night. Even though giving or selling liquor to them was highly illegal. They were far from the reservation up north and this was a good place to stay warm for the night.

Things were looking somewhat perilous to this New Yorker. After all, I still had my last twelve dollars stuffed far down in a pocket. One Navajo immediately passed out flat on the bench opposite me. His now hiked up Levi pants legs gave me my first introduction to a pair of real cowboy boots! They were wildly yellow colored with white and green leather patterns. Carved leather tooling designs of black and green stitching, depicting flying eagles, adorned the shanks and feet. Long, green, "Mule-Ear" leather straps, hung down on each side, to be used to pull the boots up and on easily. Wearing pointed, high heeled boots marked them all as horsemen. To this day, these were the prettiest boots I ever did see.

When they saw me raise up and stretch they smiled and grunted in their guttural Navajo dialect. I smiled back in reserved astonishment. I learned their greeting phrase was Yo-Ta- Hey Shaadony. Nervously, I dug out my cigarettes and offered them a smoke. That even got the attention of the sleeper. All three then crowded around me to accept a smoke. The *Peace-Pipe* now lit.

Guess I was just as strange to them as they were to me. Even in their inebriated condition they were polite and friendly. I relaxed and accepted our strained palaver. However, our conversation was severely handicapped. I didn't speak 1949 tipsy Navajo and they sure didn't understand Brooklyneze.

I showed them my Engineers boots which were also rugged in their own way, but terribly ugly. I then got to view all three pairs of their fine boots proudly displayed. It was apparent they spent all their money just like all cowboys do. First on hats, boots and then booze. (Well... Women were too hard to come by in those parts then.) We spent an hour or so of pointing and hand-gesturing until my bus came.... The first time I had set foot in Arizona and I was already thrilled down to the bone. Knowing I was really now in the "WEST!"

BUS TO COTTONWOOD

I settled on the right side in a window seat of a practically empty bus... and soon slumped fast asleep. After a few miles the rocking bus began careening down Oak Creek Canyon. Not just any canyon, but a grand-daddy of all high, snowy, twisting, glorious scenic chasms. This steep, crooked, narrow road is not something to be quickly introduced to if you have never, ever, traveled even one canyon before.

The lurch of the bus around a hair-pin switch-back bounced my head from the window I had been using for my pillow. On the return blow I woke up to, again, launch back from the window. Because there before me was a view most spectacular for this city boy! I was looking straight down... to see in the moonlight... the tops of snow covered Ponderosa pine trees.

Yes! "The Tops, I say!"... Who could sleep now? I thought... *Mom, this ain't New York anymore!*

I remained wide awake because Arizona, with God's assistance greeted me now in this special way. Although I have since traveled that road hundreds of times I still admire Oak Creek Canyon very much. If you'd like to envision this more, then read Zane Grey's vivid descriptions in his novel, *Call Of The Canyon.*

MOUNTAIN VIEWS

Later years, during spring/summer, I rode fence for the DK Ranch from their mountain line camp at Timothy Patch cabin. For fifty years this long fence line often brought me out to this canyons western towering cliff points. Far above that highway 89A, up where fences are not necessary. Rugged cliffs made the boundaries of grazing for the cattle. Out on those rocky precarious bluffs, alligator juniper trees grow with such great trunks, you could hide your horse behind them. Trees, some now old as the time of Christ.

I'd carry a can of fruit for lunch... maybe a biscuit with bacon. Sometimes just a pocket full of Jerky, something to share with my dog. The hobbled horse would rest and graze. Man, Horse and Dog, quietly together, on the edge of their world. Gazing down at the occasional traffic winding its way up and down that civilized trail. Looking much like my childhood's little toy autos.

So next time you're driving up to Flagstaff on 89A, keep looking high, high up on your left... Some future springtime you may see little tiny specks up there. It could be me, my horse, and dog, having lunch or a nap up there again... Someday...

COTTONWOOD

Next morning the bus stopped at the town of Cottonwood. I awoke, stiffly and disembarked. Later learned the bus had already past the desolate dirt road to my future mail-order job. Even if I had been awake, eleven miles back, I wouldn't have known that anyhow. Cottonwood was enjoyably quaint, and interesting. Everything was old-fashioned right down to the hitching post in front of Tumbleweeds Saddle Shop at the lower end of this four street town. At towns center was a drug store where you could also buy ice cream sodas.

COTTONWOOD STREETS

Everyone I met on the street said a smiling "Good Morning." All seven of them! I liked these folks and inquired of a few as to the exact location of the Spring Creek Ranch. Everyone knew this ranch because it was known to be a lion (cougar) hunting ranch. What? Lions? This was news to me. My mind turned back to Tarzan and Frank Buck... I was unafraid. After all, I'd seen it all, in those Saturday, eleven cent, New York movie matinees.

I easily hitchhiked a ride eleven miles back northward to the Spring Creek Ranch. Saying my thanks I stepped out on a lonesome highway with much apprehension and excitement. I walked briskly and determinedly down a dusty ranch road on the trail to my cowboy future. Just me, a little black suitcase of belongings, with twelve dollars left in my pockets.

It must have been a mile or so to the ranch on this arid desert path. Tall Cottonwood trees off to the left marked the beginning of Spring Creek bubbling up from the earth. I became overcome with a strange peaceful feeling of being completely at home among these drastically new surroundings. Arizona magically charmed and accepted me, as I did her. I knew I had made the proper choice.

The pure creek spring water sparkled a welcome addition to these surroundings. Bursting from the ground to flow many miles into Oak Creek, then on to the larger Verde River. The long downhill miles of Mooney

Canyon reached here, now to begin their new name, Spring Creek. At times, because of flash flooding, it ran for days like a high raging, uncrossable river. Easily rolling trees and huge boulders, it brought Flagstaff's melted snow to the valley. But most of the year I learned it to be so comfortably serene and beautiful. It's shading Cottonwoods lining the streams banks, where watercress grew plentiful and waited for my salads.

Small river rock and flagstone built cabins began to appear off to my left. I walked on uphill to the largest one. It was pleasantly silent all that way. Even with the darting about of a few jackrabbits here and there it seemed so very quiet to this seventeen-year-old city kid. When I got close to the big cabin I noticed someone on a short ladder painting a window jamb. A trim young woman in her late twenties with her back to me as I spoke a "Hello." She turned to look me over with a question in her gaze.

I said, "I'm the guy you hired, George Fischer, from New York."

She just nodded and painted a few more strokes while I looked about for some sign of what I saw depicted in those shoot 'em up western movies I often watched back home. Galloping steeds, dust, spurs a jingling, etc...

I asked, "Where are all the Cowboys?"

She casually turned, grinned and said, "You're It!"

This Spring Creek Ranch was only a 100 acre hunting ranch with small numbers of livestock. I had seen *real ranches* in the movie Red River last year, but I was not deterred. This was a foothold to my dream!

I soon learned I had two bosses, Leo and Shirley. At times, they both wore six-guns. Leo displayed two glistening.44 caliber pearl handled pistols. Shirley, just one long-barreled.38. They kept the coyote population around the ranch to a minimum.

I tirelessly fantasized... *When would I, too, be a cowboy?*

Coyotes Tears

I'm just a coyote who ranges alone
I must move on and on lest my presence be known
By those who would hurt me and invade my home
So I'm doomed forever to roam... just roam

I wander over the great Southwest
To you I seem free! Just another roving pest
But, tho' I'm a gypsy by every action and deed
Sorrow grows in my heart like a terrible weed

Each day brings new sadness, for I'm hated by all
Even cast out by my own... Who each night I call
As I cry in the moonlight, my muzzle to the sky
I wonder... who else... feels the same as I?

Aren't we all, somehow, the same in a way?
Don't we all look for happiness day after day?
So if I should awaken you in the dead of some night
With a mournful how lab out my plight...
Think of me as your heart... cryin' that night!

Leo and Shirley both kept me real busy. Shirley occasionally helped with the livestock chores, but I inherited all the cleaning of the cabins, including the coed bathroom/shower cabin, too. I also had to continually hoe out all the weeds that infested the many crooked gravel paths. Those winding trails led from the barn to each of the cabins and on up to the main building. The big house had a large bedroom and office were Leo resided. Scattered in that big cabin were bathrooms, showers, a pantry, kitchen, even a very large walk-in freezer and meat locker. That locker stored all our fresh meat, as well as Trophy game, heads, antlers and hides carefully stored for any guest hunters.

Without exaggeration, the enormous dining room impressed all who dined there. It had a fireplace at each end of its long extraordinarily decorated room. Fireplaces large enough to roast an entire four hundred pound hog, or a cowhands favorite choice of beef, the entire hind quarter of a steer.

All the partially paneled rock walls had various mounted heads of game. Elk, deer, cougar, bear, and bison from Arizona. Plus African lion, tiger, gazelle, and other deer like heads with unusual antlers. Hung between these were valuable oil paintings depicting phases of this man's entire life of hunting big game. The center of that long room was filled by a sturdy, lengthy, hardwood dining table. It easily seated twelve dinner guests at it's glistening, shapely carved and polished top. During most winter evenings we dined by firelight from both cavernous fireplaces.

Before reaching the dining area you had to pass the meal prep and dish washing stations with a well supplied cooking area privately off to one side.

"Private" it was because of the little sawed-off, short-tempered, cleaver wielding

Chinese cook who owned that kitchen and everything in it. Once, I got him mad (not angry, but mad) with my teasing and he chased me all the way back to my cabin. Wielding his razor sharp cleaver and angrily imbedding it, twice, in the protective, wooden door I desperately was holding shut! Lucky for me, he had to get right back to his cooking. I walked on eggs around him then for a week. You just can't imagine how wild it sounds to be cussed out in Chinese.

Ranch livestock consisted of nine horses, five mules, three cows, two calves, five pigs with piglets, and some chickens. Not by anybody's standards, a large cattle ranch, but still plenty western for this city dude. After much coaching by Shirley, I soon did all the livestock chores by myself, before breakfast. It was not entirely a poor choice of western ranch employment. During the almost ten months I worked there I learned many tricks and trades useful to my future horse and cattle career. It certainly helped that I had rode plenty of farm and park rental horses for two or three prior summers back east.

CHAPTER FIVE

Up To The Hunting Grounds

Let me help you grasp the full picture of our hunting trips. Spring Creek Ranch only served as the base for this much sought after hunting ranch. People from all over the world came to central Arizona to hunt wild game in this mountainous wild country. The base ranch was located at about a 3,200 foot elevation. To hunt the big game involved traveling seventy miles by truck to Bunker Hill Cabin.

HUNTING GROUNDS

Near the wilderness area of Sycamore Canyon, that was up in the 7,000 foot elevations of the Mogollon rim. A large, well equipped ranch truck provided us with the means to carry seven or eight horses, camping supplies and other gear. Even cages were installed underneath for the hunting dogs.

Additional gear had to be packed (by you know who) on a mule train from the lower ranch up high into the mountains created by the Mogollon Rim. That treacherous trail led up to Bunker Hill by way of the steep, winding Mooney Trail. A trip of about a thirty five mile short-cut to the far away Bunker Hill cabin. It's a long all day job a-horseback, leading four or five mules behind you, all lashed together in single file. This made a long pack string, tied head-to-tail, that these horses and mules were accustomed to. Charlie Russell's painting, *When Mules Wore Diamonds,* is a wonderful reference to this.

Always an exciting, scenic, hour-after-hour ride while watching and checking our packs. Constantly, carefully, being alert that your lead rope to the first mule, held in your hand, is never dropped, or even worse, gets under your own horses tail. That's an immediate bucking horse ride during which you have to dally (wrap) your lead rope around your saddle horn to hold it hard and fast. Then moving quickly ahead will jerk the rope out from under your horses clamped down tail and he will quit pitching! If you, instead, let it slide all the way thru, the now clamped down tail area, that rope will burn your horses tail badly. This could spoil a horse from future work like this. All this commotion done while climbing a narrow trail less than two foot wide. Winding along with a mountain wall almost straight up on your left and a long tumble down to the right. This sometimes makes for a chilly trip on a hot Arizona afternoon.

Mostly we traveled north, with the last four miles leading to the east. Bunker Hill cabin was on the very edge of the rim. At dark you could walk out on the mountains edge and see a few dim lights far, far out below. Some were about eighty miles out as the crow flies. Squint hard and spot a few faint lights of the 1949 town of Cottonwood over sixty miles away. Directly below, maybe twenty miles as the eagle glides, gleamed one lone light down in the depths of Oak Creek Canyon. During the day you could see a small part of a large tin roof reflecting sunlight there. That night light was on the old skating rink building along highway 89A seven miles north of Sedona. Read Zane Grey's novel *Call Of The Canyon* for more about that marvelous chasm.

With an introduction like all this, to Arizona's landscapes, I knew I was never again to be a city-dweller. Never to be a "nine to fiver" subway rider. But now, unwittingly, I had become a "five to niner", which most of the time are ranchers hours.

My very first introduction to Bunker Hill camp will always be a very memorable trip. Since I arrived at this job as such a Brooklyn green-horn I initially rode up in the truck with Leo to Bunker Hill cabin for my initial orientation. Shirley and a newly hired broncstomper took the pack train up that day. Junior, the new hand, was mostly hired to tame and train two bucking horses that Leo could not control. An ornery sorrel mare, named Iodine and a steel blue roan named, of course, Blue Steel. Shirley and I called them Blue and Iodine. Leo and Junior had other, more colorful names for them. These half-trained horses were not quiet enough for these trips so they remained back at the valley ranch.

DEEP IN SYCAMORE CANYON

CHAPTER SIX

A Glance At My Future

Now, I must tell about a very defining conversation with Leo on my first long drive up to the mountain hunting camp at Bunker Hill cabin. Leo had accepted me as help because I was a diligent, dependable worker.

I found out today he never once thought I'd become a cowhand. Just made sure I earned every bit of that forty a month he was supplying. Seven days a week, ten hours every day, but I think I got the best of Leo because of how much I would regularly eat. Leo's Chinese cook, with his meat-cleaver-assisted temper, could sure rustle up great chuck.

I tried to stay on the good side of him and he was determined to fatten up my 132 pounds. I wasn't in this adventure for the forty dollars a month anyway, and kept this in mind.

ROGERS LAKE

Along about a little over half way on this drive we passed Flagstaff and entered into the Ponderosa pine and oak tree forest. We were now on the range of the DK, Coconino Cattle Company. To my surprise we came upon the open meadows of Rogers Lake.

It was late spring 1949 and that ranch had driven most of their cattle up that same Mooney Trail. Near two thousand head of their cattle were already scattered and grazing up in these mountains. Now out on that two square miles of mostly dry lake bed I saw my first real cattle ranch! From the road we were following into the forest we could look out across that lake and see big hereford steers dotting the scene by the hundreds. Fat, healthy and pretty they were. I gazed intently at everything. Across the lake, far away, you could see the distant ranch buildings like a little toy town.

Three homes, a bunkhouse, two shops, a large barn with many corrals, and even a round corral for starting their broncos. I could even see many colorful horses grazing those ranch pastures. Farther out in the distance rose the fascinating, magnificent 14,000 foot, snow-capped San Francisco Peaks. Good Golly! What a picture I saw. What a picture I was almost in!

I practically shouted out, "Look! Look, Leo, there's where I want to work. On a ranch like that one! A real cattle ranch! Horses, cattle, cowboys, and all!"

Leo's response was stinging but made no impression on my determined mind. "You? He chuckled... Shucks, they only hire REAL cowboy's to ride for that there brand!"

SAN FRANCISCO PEAKS 14,000 feet

That was 1949 and neither of us knew what would evolve later in the spring of 1954. After almost five years, a multitude of cowpunchin' jobs and a stint with the US Marines in Korea...it transpired to another spring and a different dusty road I then went down. Traveling to the Windmill Ranch winter Headquarters of the Coconino Cattle Co. Also called the DK. To hire out for a job that lasted over fifty years. Thirty-five of which I was their foreman and ranch manager. I ain't braggin'. Just wishin' ole Leo coulda known about it all before he died!

CHAPTER SEVEN

A-Hunting We Will Go

We finally arrived at Bunker Hill to set up camp for our lion hunting guests. They followed us there in a rented Jeep.

DK RANCH SUMMER CORRALS

Three gentleman from Pennsylvania. Friendly and rugged they were, but just as green as I was to this wild unknown country. Shirley and Junior soon showed up with the pack string and extra mounts.

We finally arrived at Bunker Hill to set up camp for our

Lion hunting guests. They followed us there in a rented jeep.

Three gentleman from Pennsylvania. Friendly and rugged they were, but just as green as I was to this wild unknown

Country. Shirley and Junior soon showed up with the pack string and extra mounts.

Leo and Junior unpacked the mules while Shirley and I took care of the dogs. They each had their own pine tree with a little dog shelter. There they were each chained and fed separately. Their only time on the loose will be when hunting. Then always under the control of Leo's commands and the large cow's horn he fashioned into a very loud beckoning instrument. He could sure blow that horn like a Hawaiian blowing a conch. I never could learn to make a sound out of the spare horns we had around his ranch. Still wish I could. I just have no musical talent at all. I can't even carry a tune in a bucket!

These hounds were always severely punished if they didn't come back when the horn was blown. Any disobediences were corrected immediately by hanging them from a tree limb, by their wide leather collar and Leo whipping them with anything handy! The number of swats to equal the extent of misbehavior. I never enjoyed that scene. Maybe that's the way it's done with these huge mean hounds...

We brought nine dogs this trip. Three of them were young and in training. An older, smarter dog did the training and a lot of the reprimanding. The young dog always paid attention because he was closely linked at the neck to the older hound. Tied collar to collar, with only the length of a large double-ended swivel snap to separate them on the hunt. The youngster learned real fast to follow the old dog everywhere, or get bitten harshly. He learned to sit, stand, run, whenever, where-ever and fast! Do as the teacher would do, or suffer his wrath.

If he refused the old hound would attack him. The bleeding youngster soon learned to obey!

Obedience was very necessary because of all the dangers and perils during a lion hunt. The eagerness of the dogs sometimes gets them killed. Besides us liking and admiring them, they were very valuable and took years to train. They all are bred to track game, but to confront a bear or cougar is taught by the intense training of certain dogs that are born with a brave heart. One blow of a bears paw could kill or cripple a dog for life. Sharp fangs and claws of a lion are always at the ready anytime a cat meets a dog! Any swipe results in a wound that needs days, even weeks, of doctoring, medicine and attention.

When hunting deer, or elk we seldom took a bunch of hounds. Just one or two for company. Always different ones so we could teach them words of praise and others of commands. These were enjoyable days because they were slower and easier on everyone. None of the animals were pressed for any kind of special performance. I think they enjoyed these days, too. Although they really relish the actual lion chases even more!

On most hunts we would carry a light lunch of some kind of a sandwich or two. I'll never forget how those hounds would watch us eat. It was so very comical. The rule was to never give them any food as long as we were sitting and eating. Any scraps were saved for when we were completely finished. Then we had to be sure to separate and feed equal amounts of scraps to the dogs we brought.

The comical part was as we sat and ate with our backs to a big Ponderosa pine. In front of us, sitting on their haunches, in a forlorn, pleading semi-circle, were these waiting hounds. Staring intently at every single bite we took! They never got a morsel until we all were finished with ours! Patiently waiting, along with a deep swallow to match, in unison, each, and every one of ours. Gulp, gulp, gone!

Evenings, back at Bunker Hill, my sunset chore, among others, was to saddle a horse and put pack saddles on two mules. Then attach two large empty metal milk can jugs, one to each side of a mule. Always in the proper measured and balanced manner. Then I headed off to the Bunker Hill Spring. It was off to the west down an easy slanting trail into a deep side canyon. The canyon got narrower and narrower, while the trail got steeper and steeper. The entire downhill trip had you looking straight off the mountain to the southwest. The clear views down thru Verde Valley went on for more than eighty smogless miles. I'd swear you could see out into next week!

DOWN TO BUNKER SPRING

When it seemed you would soon ride clear off the edge, a cement water trough appeared near the trailside. Behind it, on the hillside, was a small fenced in area with a metal covered puddle at its center. Protruding from under that lid was a piece of pipe that ran a thin stream of cool spring water into that gently running over trough. A perfect place to sit, admire the view, and contemplate your day, or your life.

Sometimes I brought a fresh apple to eat there before supper. Idly tossing the core anywhere. I rode back there about ten years later, as it was on the DK Ranch range and found a fine producing apple tree nearby that spring. One of my very few successes at farming.

They were waiting for water back at camp so I pulled off the lids to the four milk cans. With an old bucket, left there for this purpose, I filled the cans with fresh spring water. The old fashioned milk cans held about fifteen gallons each. Two cans on each mule, I now had acquired almost sixty gallons, minus a little sloshing out on the uphill return trip. It would supply the camp for a day or so. The evening ride back was pleasantly enjoyed by the occasional sighting of deer also coming down for a drink. Once I even saw a rare albino deer. Only once in over fifty-five years.

CHAPTER EIGHT

The Cougar Capture

The guests, three Pennsylvania gentlemen, are eager to bag a lion. We rose before dawn and went about getting prepared for a long day in the wilds of nearby Sycamore Canyon.

We hope to cross trails down there, somewhere , with a roaming cougar. They, too, are out hunting, but unaware we have dogs with excellent noses to pick up their scent.

A 1949 Arizona lion easily weighs over a hundred and ten pounds. Living entirely on a diet of plentiful venison and young cattle. The ranchers would be happy to know there may be one less today.

They even paid a hundred dollar bounty if you'd show them a fresh dead cougar.

COUGAR TREED

I and the hunting guests are just extra baggage for now. Leo is in entire control of men and dogs. We ride along quietly chatting and waiting. Leo is intent to satisfy his hunter customers. He watches the dogs trailing and sniffing. Listening to other dogs that are ahead but out of sight. Maybe barking in chase, or baying if they corner or tree something. It's just old hat for Shirley, so she has remained in camp. It's a long hot morning, and we carry only a little water to go around. Soon, we'll be at

Winter Cabin where another spring runs clear
and we can drink, rest and fill canteens.

WINTER CABIN PHOTO, CREDIT TO KRIEG:

A short stop there lets us reconnoiter. The
hunters check their rifles, pistols and
ammunition. Leo only carries his two pearl-
handled .44 caliber six-shooters. It's our first
day, and we don't expect much. Neither do the
hounds because they are back around us now.
Crowding around us to see if we are already
eating the lunch Shirley made for us this early
A.M. That's how hunting days go. Boring and
exciting all at the same time. Still, any lion is

only a fresh scent away from this ambitious pack of noses.

We press on, down into the jagged lower trails, stringing along the high boundaries of the eastern Sycamore Canyon sides. The deep canyon views are astounding and the hunters cameras click like crickets. Suddenly the old lead dog sprints off and barks ferociously. The others need no other cue... they are off running and sniffing. A chorus of excited yelping echoes around canyon walls, as we swiftly trot to keep up. Loping on those trails is almost impossible. Especially with riders not familiar with narrow canyon trails.

The dogs leave the trail and begin to climb out and up the canyon side. Leo urgently gives me the reins to his mount and follows the dogs a-foot. In some spots he even boosts a crawling dog or two up over boulders. It's a tough sweaty chase for him, but he is as determined as the dogs are. The other hunters also abandon their horses and mules to follow Leo. The gaps between lion, dogs and men are closing up.

A little confused as to what to do next, I decide not to lose our mounts and lead Leo's mule while the others sorta follow. Making a circular winding trip I listen for the dogs, now baying in the distance. I continued to wind around towards their sounds. The other mounts follow along slowly, as they are often hindered by stepping on their own long reins. That's when long reins are helpful. Makes it easier to catch a loose horse.

LION TRAPPED

When reaching the noisy, dusty, jumble of activity I saw the dogs had treed a young cougar in a small oak tree. Leo and the three hunters have also just made their climb up the hill. Pictures are being taken while a discussion arises as to who's shot is to take the lion down.

Jokingly, it is suggested, to *"Capture him alive,* like Frank Buck would in the jungle."

Leo chimes in, assessing the situation. Stating that it is not a full grown lion and if we all agree to assist it may be possible. We take a vote to all pitch in while the cougar is the only one to abstain. Time is running out because the lion will soon bolt out of the tree and take his chances of escaping the hounds. For now he catches his breath, feeling safe from the yelping, jumping, circling dogs.

When a child, have you ever tried to grab a good sized, five pound cat and stuff him in a sack to be transported? You probably still remember the wild scramble and scratches you suffered all over your body? Well this is about the same only now much multiplied with a ninety pound kitty.

Leo has found a slim dead jack-pine tree and attached his lariat to an end. Leaving open a sizable loop to hopefully slip over the cat's head. We secure another lasso to Leo's to be sure we have plenty of rope to work with when the cat leaves the tree. To carefully raise the pole and slip the noose over the confused cougars head now seems to have been the easiest part of this entire capture. I have helped catch raccoons the same way with the Self boys so I'm thinking it is almost the same. Raccoons, too, can put up a terrific fight with a painful bite and sharp claws. This event was a frightfully exaggerated repeat of all that.

When that noose tightened around that lion's neck he left the tree with a screeching, snarling squall sounding like a mad women's scream. He hit the dirt with a snarl at the hounds and was off in an instant. Only to be brought up short by Leo's lasso wrapped around a nearby small pine. As the cat rolled, jumped, and struggled, three of us on the rope gradually drew him up tight to the tree. Choking, spitting and snarling at the surrounding dogs, he was still all pointed claws and teeth.

I rounded up the excited hounds and necked them together where possible. Then tied them out of the way. We were hurrying, stumbling and falling over each other to safely subdue this tornado of a fur-ball. We must subdue all this thrashing about by catching the hind feet. A rope around the lions flanks made us able to stretch him out and fasten other lines to each hind foot. We then attached those sharp dangerous paws to each other. Front paws were next, but first we had to be able to avoid his fangs.

Leo picked up a dried solid oak stick off the ground and broke it off short in the fork of a tree. After a try or two he ended up with about twelve inches of strong oak a little thicker than a broom handle. Next we each snared a front paw with a looped rope to pull the claws away from the cat's head, still secured to the unforgiving pine tree. While immobilized in this position the cat could not scratch, or bite Leo when he bravely put that stick in the cougar mouth. Anxious to get at us, the cougar bit down on the stick and fearless Leo quickly began to wrap figure-eights of leather dog leash around the stick and the lions muzzle. Now that cat could still breath thru his nose and mouth, but not open his jaws. I've done the same, though with only little pet coyotes and raccoons.

The five of us struggled with securing the front feet together same as the hind feet. Our five mounts had to donate half of their doubled saddle blankets to the cause. A bandana blindfold took a lot of fight out of the cat. We wrapped the head separately. The hind feet tied together making a total of three safe wraps all in spare blankets. I and one guest were the only one riding a horse that day, Leo rode his best mule. We had to decide which of the remaining mules would tolerate carrying the subdued lion. Leo knew his mules well from other hunts. It takes a sensible, older, trusting mule to allow a lion on his back. Leo knew which one had best allowed dead and bloody game hoisted up on his back before. The best rider of the hunting guests was picked to lead that mule and I gave my horse to the hunter left afoot. I had to make that long trail back to Bunker Hill riding double behind Leo. It was a successful, good day and we were elated and proud.

"Shucks, Frank Buck ain't got nothin' on us!" We all proclaimed.

At camp we transferred the cougar to the largest dog cage before completely untying him. There he spent the night. Leo and Junior took him back to the Spring Creek Ranch the following morning. There waited a very large lion's cage. Built for this sole purpose, close by the dog pen. Cougars never get friendly, or settled. Only, ever-enduringly, pace or stalk back and forth in their cage. Leo eventually sold him to the Phoenix Zoo.

We had a restful lazy next day at camp waiting for them to return. Tomorrow we'll try to bag a trophy from that lion family that is probably in that same area. Those hunters already have a big wild yarn to carry back to Pennsylvania. I bet in a month or so that captured lion grew, in their minds, from 90 to 190 pounds, as would their entire rendition of the chase.

Days later we continued the hunt until the guests finally shot another lion to take home. That fall they were back to hunt elk. All three men were successful then. Leo always provided a fortunate outcome for his guiding and hunting trips. Making each day comfortable for his regular guests. I, too enjoyed it all... But still yearning for that range cowboy life... Months later I met the Selfs and my quest then took a better turn.

CHAPTER NINE

The Self Family

At Spring Creek Ranch I worked for nearly nine months. There I learned much about riding, roping, packing mules, capturing lions, bad horses and those were the easy lessons! It was while out scouting the range for some of the ranches livestock.... I first met the Self boys...

I was riding one of the ranches spoiled bucking horses that day. Out searching the range for some of the ranches mules, horses and our milk cow. It was customary to take a rideable bronc out of the training corrals as soon as possible. However, Leo opened the corral gate many days too soon for the mare, Iodine and I to be leaving the ranch. Just because this New York greenhorn was aboard this unpredictable spoiled horse it didn't mean he was a capable broncobuster.

"Go try to bring back the milk cow, George," Leo hollered, as I cautiously left the safety of the bronc pen.

I had demonstrated for a week or two that I could manage this half broke horse. I usually could pull up her head when she tried to buck me off. In the confines of the bronc pen, that is. So I ambitiously rode off to do what cowboys do. Iodine had her own ideas about this. If I was experienced I would have detected her constant appraisal of her riders balance and my much too loose riding style. Also, un-noticed by me, was the slight hump in her back and her hesitant gait...

We managed almost two safe miles with not a horse, mule, or cow in sight. I listened for the sound of the bell that hung from the cow's neck. Up ahead, a quarter of a mile or so, I spied a pickup out in the brush. Outside that truck a man was gathering mesquite wood, for cooking I supposed. I aimed to ask him if he had seen a cow wearing a bell. As we trotted his way I noticed behind my saddle, hung on each side, was a small saddle-bag.

Foolishly, I wondered, *What would Iodine do if just raised one bag up and let it flop back down on her side?*

I did just that and with that surprise slap on her hide she lunged into a high leap as her head disappeared from in front of me. My long seven foot reins sizzled thru my hand. I reached with the other hand to grasp what was left of my only salvation. Only two inches of reins were sprouting from both clenched fists.

Her two ears appeared only briefly between the pitches. Flying across the brush we bounded past the astounded Mexican man. Our wide wild eyes met at the same time as Iodine and I narrowly missed him and his pickup by inches. His gaze, in surprised fright...mine in determination. I'm a cowboy now and will not be unseated!

On we went across the thick mesquite. Breaking it into pieces for the astonished man to gather. Bounding past, I hollered out a loud "excuse me" and the last I saw of him he was standing like a pillar of salt, wondering..."What the hell was that went by?"

I was learning even riding a bronc can hurt as much as falling off one. She made at least fifteen rough pounding jumps before giving it up... for awhile. This caused such pain as if I was being hammered and split in two. Inexperienced bronc riding usually finds you going *against* the pounding instead of actually riding the jumps. Everything in my new life was important to me. I mentally totaled the jumps she made trying to unseat me that day. It was well over forty bucks! More than equal to my wages number of...also forty bucks...a month. That evening I could hardly walk. However, try as she did that day, she never got me off!

It came for me to realize that she wisely knew how to try dumping me every time we followed a downhill trail. A bronc pitching downhill can easily generate a lot of speed, power and altitude going down a slope. I was learning!

So, I tried to make it back to the ranch by never going down any steep hillsides. I wanted to get back and get my gentle horse, Cherry and find the milk cow with him. I'd never find that cow looking just at Iodine's head and ears for a beginning warning of the next rodeo. However, those ears now were pointing to a few riders up ahead.

We came abreast, and pulled up. It was three of the five Self boys. Spooks, Howard, and Alvie. They were riding two mules and one horse. Alvie rode the filly, and the other two boys rode the mules. The grey mule, rode by Spooks, was a spooky sort. Spooks lost his real name, Lloyd, when he was very young. He always insisted on going outside in the dark to play. Howard was forking a heavy built dark mule. Their mules were used at home to pull wagons, plows, disks and other farm implements.

I guessed them boys to be younger than me. Spooks was the oldest, maybe fifteen, then Howard, thirteen and Alvie, around eleven. Clinton, the oldest was still over in Korea.

Melvin, the youngest at about seven, was at home. I needed this rest, and they were happy to visit with a fellow rider. The fact of this new and sprouting friendship to be is that, even to this very day, we are all still as close as brothers could ever be.

They soon found out I hailed from New York and our conversation grew. We had much in common with interests in livestock, ranching and anything "cowboy." My desire to be a real cowboy thrilled them. They said their dad Jess would help me. I, in turn, told them how I was working for small wages and that it was not a big ranch as I had envisioned it to be. Not a place for real cowboys. They sympathized with my trapped plight and quickly invited me to stay with them anytime I had the urge to quit my job for a better one.

That was 1949 and to this day these boys still argue as to; Who saw me, met me, talked to me first! Well I don't even know myself. I learned to love them all the same. Their two older sisters, Irma, and Mildred were so graciously lovely and friendly, too. To this day, anyone around those parts named Self is loved, trusted, and respected.

Their father, Jess, was part Texas Indian, as his mom was mostly all Comanche. She lived in the nearby hills and tended sheep and goats until she died at well over 100. But the Queen of this entire brood was the children's mother, Sylvia. Everyone called her Mom Self because she cared for and mothered just about all who came around her. It is easy to see where all the sweetness and goodness came from to abide in this big family.

MOM SELF

Mom Self took me in like one of her own. Even though she already had a big family she still had room for this New York vagabond. They just don't make folks like that, anymore. My days around this Self family will always be an unforgettable happy place in a special corner of my mind.

Sylvia Self was a sweet, kind hearted, hard working ranch Mom. Always fussing around her wood-fired cook stove. Continually preparing meals for her husband Jess and all us boys, too.

She sure raised a fine brood. I can still taste her early morning flap-jacks with sugar syrup, strips of crispy bacon and a sunny side up egg or two...depending on Alvie's chickens. We ate breakfast only after we did all the morning chores.

There I always stayed between cowboy ranch jobs that they always found for me. Five boys, two big sisters and I helped all we could around that small creekside ranch. There was plenty to do on seventy plus acres, to keep the land producing. Most of it done with our bare hands, old tools and mules. The young Self boys worked the ranch before and after school hours.

Sister Irma was soon to marry a man fresh back from WW Two. Tom Mulcaire was in the Sea-Bees and cleared the jungles, built roads and airfields all over the Pacific.

He returned to Arizona to start a large construction business. He brought the first D7 Caterpillar bulldozers to the Verde Valley.

Started his business digging dirt water tank catches all over Arizona by the hundreds. Providing water to supply both game and livestock. Water that all the ranchers paid for. Irma and Tom and raised two boys, and a girl.

Then along about 1951, the younger, caring, sweet sister, Mildred, married a pole climbing Lineman. P.D. Patton was his name and they had a boy who could really play them spoons. This Self family just grew and grew. A finer bunch of down-home people you could ever meet and everyone of them also musically inclined.

Seems like every night there was a hoe-down of a gathering at the Self home. A little home built of smooth river-rock gathered up in a mule drawn wooden wagon from the nearby stream called Oak Creek. Their music resounded all up and down this little creekside foot-tappin' community.

MELVIN'S CHIP BOX

Once all we boys had a conversation about shares in the ranch. Just a comical discussion about our hard work producing stuff around the place for all to make a few dollars with. Howard, who sang all the time, spoke up and said he had a sizable herd of sheep and how he could sell some of them someday. Alvie talked about all his colorful banty, he called them, (bantam) chickens. Some of them were fighting chickens, too. He was proud of all the eggs he fed us every morning. Alvie always had a guitar in his arms. Spooks (Lloyd) was the family banjo pickin' cowman. He and I took care of the three cows we milked every morning. Plus we fed the one steer, the horse and the two mules they had, while Howard fed the sheep. Spooks could maybe sell that steer.

Anyway, little Melvin was very small and young. When it came his turn to recite what he was worth around the ranch we noticed he was just standing there, crying, while waiting for his turn to chime in about making spare money.

You'd have to know, that Jess sure liked his coffee and he drank it all day long when he was home. Us boys had our share of coffee, too. But, even to make just one pot of coffee you had to have lots of little pieces of wood to stoke the wood stove with. Plus lots of kindling for Mom Self to start up the fire roaring... Melvin was in charge of the Chip/Kindlin' Box. It was his daily chore to always keep the chip box full of wood scraps. He gathered them from around where we older boys chopped all the wood. Plus lots of little kindling for Mom Self to start the fire roaring.

Melvin just bawled and said, "Shucks, all I got is this dang chip-box."

However, he did turn out to be the best darn Auto Mechanic in the entire Verde Valley. Later, to be acclaimed the fourth best in California, and third best in Colorado!

CHAPTER TEN

My Last Speech Lesson

One morning stands out hilariously funny at my own expense. I vowed never to make this mistake again. The Self family really knew how to laugh, and tease each other. Mostly they enjoyed teasing me about my Brooklyn street slang accent. On our usual early mornin' trip to the barn we were finishing up our numerous chores. Spooks, Alvie, and I were almost done milking the three milk cows. We always made a race of this last chore. They hollered at me from their separate stanchions, asking if I was almost done milking my cow yet.

I replied, to my doom...

"Yeah! I just got a few more squoits left."

Well that was the beginning of a never ending rant of teasing about my entire Brooklyn way of talking. Yes, they laughed about it before, but now it was hitting home to their ranch activities and fair game for criticism. I was now destined to be called out on each and every New York twang in my speech.

So from that day on ...I was very careful to not slip and say anything like boid, thoid, shoit, or even horse toid, again. I was also very careful not to "choin" the butter anymore, or step off a street "coib" in town. When working, we never got any "doit" on us either. I never realized I had acquired such a curse, and they were determined to rid me of it. To this day, I catch myself when I almost make those Dead End Kids, street gang, slip-ups with any of my woids. Whoops! I meant words! *I'm still hearing those friendly taunts, jeers and laughs.*

We boys had quite a time together along the banks of Oak Creek.. Mostly learning everything the hard way. Jess worked long hard days "Skinning Cat" as we called operating the D7 Caterpillar bulldozer. The ranch responsibilities were up to us boys. Irrigating crops and alfalfa fields was very important. There was much livestock to take care of, too. A herd of sheep, three milk cows, sometimes with calves, chickens of all kinds, a few hogs and of course, cats and dogs. I always thought I was now in my special Heaven.

It wasn't all work. We fished day and night, swam in Oak Creek, chased raccoons with hounds at night and hunted deer on House Mountain. It was exciting fun chasing the dogs as they ran raccoons in the dark of the night. We carried flashlights to keep from stumbling and falling when at a dead run. Soon the raccoon was tired, the dogs had it treed. All yapping excitedly in unison, underneath. Little Melvin had his one job. It was now up to him to climb the tree to the raccoons safe limb. To shake that branch vigorously until the raccoon fell out commencing another ruckus of a chase. I remember little Melvin fell from the tree, once, and the dogs pounced on him viciously, not realizing, it was just little Melvin, the chip box kid.

CHAPTER ELEVEN

Ranch To Ranch

My numerous stays in my adopted family and home were a blessing from above. True to their promise, the boy's father Jess, kept me working on local cattle ranches. Time passed as I worked for almost all the large ranches around the Verde Valley. I was literally learning the *ropes,* plus the bridles, bits, saddles, etc.. The biggest spreads were the V bar V (V-V) and the M Diamond. (✗)   Their Buckhorn Mountain roundup camps were side by side, up on the summer grazing country. Separated only by a barbed-wire fence.

All the cowhands worked together for both ranches at the same time. As was done years ago, with wide open range land, mixed owners and brands. During those bygone days "rodeo" was born. Daily we had lots of cowboy labor, fun and competition, too. Sleeping scattered out all around in our bedrolls, under the jillion nightly stars.

There at the M Diamond Ranch I became good friends with Enoch Walker. We both were working for Irvin Walker at his M Diamond Ranch. Years later Enoch always invited me to rodeo with him. Even offered to pay my bull riding entry fees because he liked the way I rode those Brahman bulls...

But I really only enjoyed being simply a range riding cowboy all year long. Enoch later became Worlds Champion Saddle Bronc Rider of 1960. I just stayed at the M Diamond.

Before spring round-up I had the pleasant job of riding up the trail we would be using to take the ranches cattle to summer country. The Hollingshead Trail. Most of the winter snow had melted and my job was to check the first two or three watering places. We had to know, in advance, where to first take the herd. At the bunkhouse that evening, I wrote this poem, to give it to Irvin at dinner

CHECKIN' ON THE WATER

When winters darn near over
and spring comes rollin' round
The cattle start to thinkin'
'bout their move to summer ground
I'll ride on up to the summer range
on a pony fast and tough
Just a-checkin' on the water
to see they've got enough
Then I'll know where to graze 'em
until the brandin's thru
And when their free 'til autumn
I'll know where their goin' to
I'll jog on by ole Painted Tank,

I'll surely find some there
That tanks set in a right nice place,
ketches water every year
Further on and up the canyon
where the deer all seem to go
There's a sorta hidden spring,
but the water is always low
Maybe this time I'll be lucky
and find a better stream
With the trough a-runnin' over!
Now I reckon that's a dream
Just a little help from Heaven
and the cows will have it fine
So I reckon I won't worry
as I go ridin' thru the pine
I'll just trot on home a-singin',
things will be all right
The long days been tiresome,
but my heart is feelin' light
Too bad I can't tell them cows,
"I went ridin' out today
Just a-checkin on the water,
Don't worry, it's Okay!"

The V-V was owned by Bruce Brocket who almost became Governor of Arizona circa 1950. They had over 300 head of horses to supply their ranch and sell to other ranchers. What a thrilling picture it was driving that colorful bunch stampeding from place to place. Manes, tails and hooves a-flying from multi-colored, almost wild horses.

On these roundups I had my first introduction to the mountain oyster delicacy. I immediately found them absolutely delicious and have since eaten hundreds. Those cooked on mesquite branding fires tasted best. Always easily available in my chosen line of employment.

We worked a short distance from the herd with two branding teams and two ropers. It was fast and furious work as those ropers seldom missed. They would try to catch the calves by both hind legs and drag them to the branding crews. Snaring a calf by only one leg was okay but considered almost a miss by a good hand. Near the fire they were branded, dehorned, ear-marked and vaccinated. The young bulls were castrated.

At the Buck Horn Mountain roundup grounds we ate those calf fries straight out of the branding fire. On a long day we worked over 150 calves with two branding crews. Almost half of them were turned into steers.

That operation provided the cocinero (cook) with a hundred or more little danglers for upcoming meals. Since then, I've consumed many pairs (they come in pairs ya know) straight from the mesquite branding fire coals and some at restaurants, too. I've given you all the details please do your own shopping and research for recipes.

DANGEROUS HORNED COW HERD

This type of work had many unusual, exciting moments. It was lots of play spiked with plenty of unplanned events. The struggling calves put up quite a battle when caught. Some born in January, it now being May or June, were approaching 400 plus pounds. The two punchers who held them down (one on the head, the other grasping both hind legs) were often dislodged, butted, stepped on and run over. Much to the laughing amusement and criticism of other hands.

The mother cow herd was never de-horned. They were kept with their horns on for protection against cougars and coyotes. Those years, if you dismounted near a cow with a calf, you'd best stand behind your horse. Cows were sorta accustomed to four legged tall animals, but always charged any two legged critters. It was dangerous to doctor or mess around with any young calf out on the range.

Here's another more life threatening event that demonstrated the bravery and respect of young cowboys for their old-timer peers. In this case it was when our boss, Irvin Walker, was roping and dragging some calves out to the branding crew. The rules were firm. If you accidentally catch a big snuffy cow you had to get your own rope off that angry sharp horned momma. There were plenty like her in that herd and old Irvin snagged one by mistake.

We respected Irvin at his age of around seventy-five and still cowboyin'. Enoch really idolized him. He wouldn't ever let Irvin go in after that loose, roped cow, even a-horseback inside that milling herd. Enoch just grabbed the that lariat dragging passed us in the dust and hand over hand he disappeared into all those horned animals. As we listened to the clacking noises of 200 pairs of horns, he popped up here or there, with his hat still on, at that cows neck and head. Hanging on to horn and rope as she drug him round thru-out the herd. Finally he got a good grip on the noose around her horns and tore the rope free. No worse for the experience he strutted over to Irvin and handed him his lasso with a grin. Irvin smiled a "Thanks" back. A smile from a respected boss, after a tough job, is a personal rainbow for a cowhand.

Roundup over? Then time for old and new friends to part as I returned to the Self home on the creek to help the boys with their ranch work. Between jobs, I was always welcome there even though it was a small home. We boys all slept in a wooden bunkhouse next to the tool shed and rock home. Telling stories until all of us were fast asleep.

When in the Marines, they safely stored my saddle, bridles, and personal gear in that Bunkhouse. There it all stayed, safely, untouched for years, until I returned from Korea in May of 1954. I was welcomed back like a son, and have remained close thru these many, many years. I am still, a brother to them all.

CHAPTER TWELVE

Marine Reflects About Arizona Ranching

Cowhands do really love their work and the ranch they happen to be working for at any chosen time. As the saying goes "They're ridin' for the Brand." Doesn't matter who is the actual Boss, Foreman, Straw Boss, Honcho, Patron, etc... They just like the work and do it. When it comes along that they *don't like it* they just immediately quit!

Our days are spent in the company of many horses. Some we call friends and others it's just our job to try to get along with and train them better so someone else can like them. We always dearly remember the likable bunch and just tolerate the broncos and rough string.

If I were to write poems about the horses I have loved I'd never finish the task. I have written many stories about horses but sadly only a few in poems.

When I was young and only been cowboyin' three years, I worked for many ranches but never had a steady job. Lots of adventurous roaming I guess. Not enough time around the same horse to really get attached. Until I worked for the M Diamond Ranch near Rimrock Arizona. I signed on early in the fall and stayed thru the following year. Later I left for the Marine Corps, soon ending up in Korea.

While there my thoughts always turned back to that ranch and my string of cow-horses. One in particular named *Lookin' Glass.* I didn't know why at the time but found out years later Irvin had named him after a Montana Blackfoot Chief. Remembering my past with this horse was a pleasant reprieve from my unpleasant daily life so unreal from the cowboy life I loved in Arizona. It prompted me to write *this poem* and it helped calm me too.

LOOKING GLASS

Sometimes I sit back
and think of days gone by
When I use to punch cows
'neath an Arizona sky
My thoughts turn to ponies
I had in my string
To ride 'em again would
make my heart sing
Far away up in the timber right now
There's a little ole horses
that could ketch any cow
The boss called him Lookin' Glass...
I'll never know why
Probably 'cause of that twinkle
he had in his eye

He weren't very big
and kinda shy of a rope
The boys all said he resembled
a large antelope
But with all the kiddin' and teasin'

they sure did realize
That my twinkle-eyed pony
was really a prize

When we gathered
and the circles were wide
The country rough
and the cows seemed to hide
My pony would find them
and his ears showed the way
Then I'd pat his smooth neck
for findin' the stray

Right now, I reckon, he has it just fine
Nothin' to do
but roam thru the cedar and pine
Waterin' in the draw
where I used to cool his back
Or grazin' on the ridge
where we found that maverick's track

But I'll bet there's a spot
in that cow-pony's heart
That's a mite empty since we had to part

I don't know if he misses me
as I now miss him
But this fall he'll be wantin'
to take them cows off the rim

When the mounts are cut out
and the extras turned loose
He'll be wonderin' why
he wasn't caught by a noose
But I'll be back... Sometime...
Don't know just when...
And we'll roundup together
just like ole pards agin.

CHAPTER THIRTEEN

Dance Night At The Old Corral

Every Saturday night we went a few miles to the local western dancehall. It was named The Old Corral. We boys always eager to go see the girls, the fights over girls, or about cowboy hats. Those were the days when each and every man and boy wore a western hat...and absolutely nobody... better not touch your gal or your sombrero! You may get another girlfriend but your hat was one of a kind!

Back in that era, fights were long, bloody, but fair. You always fought outdoors, followed by a cheering, jeering crowd. You could give up, anytime you wanted to by saying, "Uncle." or "Okay, I've had it!".

You never hit or kicked a man that was down and never used a weapon. Usually, later, before closing time, you were seen shaking hands with your opponent and laughing about it all. Few grudges lasted very long among these similar types of friendly ranching folk.

Only food, beer and wine was sold there. Who knows what might be available in the multitude of cars and pickups that surrounded the building on three sides? I'm happy to say, there were never any drugs in use by these country folks.People from far and wide, drove to this area, fondly named after one of its first founders, Cornville. People of all ages danced to local Western music bands until one AM. Many then had to drive back home to Flagstaff, Prescott, or further. Often over sixty - seventy miles or more away.   The "Old Corral" remained a very popular Saturday night event drawing this crowd for almost forty years.

JUST ANOTHER SATURDAY NIGHT

One Saturday night, Enoch was driving us back to the M Diamond from the dance at 2:00 A.M. He and I were working for that ranch together then and had to be back at work this Sunday morning at 7:00 a.m. We were hurrying to catch a little shut-eye before saddling up. The radio was playing our favorite western tunes from Clint, Texas. The only country station strong enough, 50,000 watts, to reach us in Arizona at that time of night. Nobody but rabbits, lizards, fools and drunks were on that crooked, twelve mile, dirt road back to the ranch that night. We comprised the latter two of that group as we zoomed crazily around every sharp turn. Suddenly Enoch's old car careened, slid and rolled over about two and a half times. Luckily we were halted by a high rocky embankment on the driver's side. No seat belts in those days but we were bronc riders and rode every jump.

AUTHOR ENJOYING A SEDONA RODEO

Everything became almost silent as nuts, bolts and car parts finally quit flying around. Dust quietly settled around us and while crawling out a window, we noticed that Enoch's car sure had a dang good radio. We both exited laughing, 'cause Clint, Texas was still faintly playing one of our favorite Eddy Arnold tunes, "The Cattle Call." We just let 'er play as we strolled away. Just another typical dance night, during the 1950s, for folks like us. It's now about a five mile stroll to saddle-up at the M Diamond Ranch. *Cattle were calling us.*

MORNING CATTLE CALL

CHAPTER FOURTEEN

Windmill Ranch

May 1954 finally began my 50+ year career as a real cowboy, foreman, and manager of a ranch that always was only a western portrait in dreams. I had just returned from Korea. The Selfs told me the Windmill Ranch was hiring for its spring roundup. I gathered up all my gear they had taken care of and made plans to visit that ranch sixteen miles away.

A few saved USMC dollars bought me a local dairy's milk delivery pickup. It was old, and looked strangely comical with its three foot extended bed. Made to carry many milk bottles for delivery every day. The price was right for my slim budget and I desperately needed transportation.

The following Monday morning I drove to the Windmill. After leaving the main highway it was seven miles of seldom cared for dirt road. Hereford steers dotted the road on both sides watching the dust-devils rise from my slow bumpy progress. Soon I was at the ranch entrance. The giant elevated water storage tank, and whirling, clattering, windmill made me certain

I was at the right place. Shucks, the only place I reckon, for the past seventeen miles or so.

WINDMILL RANCH HORSES

I now entered a scene right out of western movies. The strong wooden cattle pens to the left had gates open, as steers trod in and out getting a drink from a long cement water trough. A few horses were tied near a ram- shackled wooded barn, where two cowboys, in the shade of the one lone tree were shoeing a horse.

One, mostly reclined in the shade giving unwanted advice and criticisms to the other! Future friends to be, the Baker boys. Brothers, J.T. Baker and Rayden, the oldest. J.T. was doin' the shoein', and most of the cussin' while the reclining Rayden did all the advisin'.

Out in the round bronc pen I saw Harry Davis working a horse to respect him and his Spanish, vaquero type, hackamore headgear and reins. All made from horses mane hair, except for the rawhide leather noseband. (bosal).

I got Harry's name from Billy Pitts who was twirling a lasso near the open barn door. He pointed me into the barn and there I met my future boss for over fifty years, Duane Miller. He was sitting indoors on the threshold steps of a somewhat, rat-proof grain room.

CLEVE COX ABOARD TONY

Another hand, Cleve Cox, was sitting in the adjacent room to the left on a bale of hay. There, amid a conglomeration of saddles, bridles, Spanish bits and spurs, he was sipping from a large bottle of Old Crow. For medicinal purposes I was told. He looked fairly well,...anyway...*well* over seventy years old.

Duane may have even been slightly ill, also. As he took a snort now and then, too. Cleve hid this medicine among the many bales of hay behind him in the rest of the barn. Hidden because there were other roundup hands also needing much, too much, medication.

Duane was sittin' and a-whittlin' on a stick with a very sharp knife. I was later to learn that everyone had a sharp knife and they showed me how to get mine that way. This knife was carried in a sheath on your belt. In any emergency this is the fastest way to get to your knife.

For a past example, when your horse happens to fall on you and pins you to the ground with your foot jammed tight in a stirrup, you can cut your cinches to let your struggling horse get up without dragging you along with him. It has been a useful tool for my entire life. Remember...Never bother to carry a dull knife.

I told Duane, the boss, I was looking for work, and he commenced to ask the all important 1954 cowboy hiring questions.

"Do you have your own saddle, bridle and rope? Do you have a bedroll? Can you shoe your own string of horses? Will you hire on for $150 dollars a month and grub?"

I could see my quick "Yes" replies had impressed him as he said, "Come back a soon as you can, and start shoeing your string." My pre-Marine Corps cowboyin' of three years on those other big spreads got me the job. I returned two days later...

JANZA

AUTHOR ON SLEWFOOT

NEW MAN TESTED

That's when I met Brown Bob. Looking back now, that horse must have been one of the oldest, laziest and safest horses on the ranch. Somehow, these cowhands were going to test my mettle that very first day of work. Duane said I could shoe horses tomorrow and Brown Bob was already shod. He gave me the task of taking five big lazy Hereford bulls to a water-hole called Black Tank.

"It'll be easy," they all said. "Just follow the main dirt road north about four miles and you'll be there. Put 'em in at the water tank, just close the gates to the pasture and water lot when you leave. Nothin' to it!"

I asked if that horse had any tricks I should know about and they assured me he was safe. So off I went. The first mile was easy and pleasant. The landscape was interestingly dotted with many different cacti. Prickly pear, Spanish bayonet, spider, and yucca, some in bloom. Scattered juniper and cedar trees were everywhere in sight. Brown Bob, and I were getting along fine, and I reckoned the bulls seemed to know their way. I just moseyed along until about 9:00 A.M.

Bulls mostly are hard to drive without a good dog or two. They have minds of their own and after awhile become immune to lariat slaps with a doubled rope. Still, I readily pursued my work pushing them along. They insisted on trotting off the road to eat the fresh flowery yucca blooms that invitingly sprouted along the way. They loved this once a year treat like a kid loves ice-cream. By ten a.m. we were all getting a little hot. A drink awaited us at Black Tank.

I am sometimes asked if I ever carried a canteen. I always answer for most cowhands.

"Why have that pesky dang thing bang and bounce along on your knee and horse all day long? Being hot and empty mostly all the time!"

We found water whenever we could or went without. After any brief shower there is good water puddled up on the ground and in rocks. If there was no rain we always had those dirt waterholes that stored rainwater. Or puddles from a past rain. Yes, there were bugs and a thin film of...shall I say slime, on the top?

If yer sayin' "Ugh! Oh! No! Not me!" Then you never have been really thirsty... yet.

We just flicked all that residue aside like the other smart animals do and drank from a little below the surface. Watch a horse drink, he always circles his nose around the top of the water to scatter the insects and then he drinks from an inch below the surface. We never drink any water that is completely bug-less. Never! That might kill you!

Also I have heard said, "Always drink upstream from the herd!"

My personal motto to live by is, "Never drink the dredges!"

Overheated bulls get cranky and pick fights. After bumping into each other for a mile or two they started to tussle. This job needed a good biting cow-dog. I was wishin' I had one. Plus, Brown Bob and I were outweighed by over a thousand pounds each. Then the worst problems began. They decided not to stick together, but go their own ways. It was all plenty of wide open country for me and Bob to sweep back and forth, over and over to, drive, drive all we could.

But, folks, let me ask ya this... "Why did it seem that just five bulls could go in about seven different directions at the same time?"

The last mile or so was a one-sided battle with Brown Bob and I getting no rest. We had to constantly trot back and forth, here and there, to keep those bulls moving at this now erratic bull/snail pace. They were still very nonchalant, but I was working up a sweat slapping them. While getting a sore throat howling insults at each bull.

Brown Bob was getting up a lather himself. There ain't much shade under these little cedar trees, either. Lucky for us, the bulls could smell the waterhole now and they perked up. We were very grateful when they lined out at a respectable pace and made for the water. The now … #@^*%s.o.b.%#*, multi-named, bulls went into the dirt waterhole up to their bellies and enjoyed the water. I spied a long cement water trough near a giant windmill with a twenty-five foot fan. My horse and I headed straight for that. A refreshing drink we now both enjoyed. I even doused myself as far as I could submerse my head and shoulders in the clear water. Pulled the saddle off ole Bob and washed his back. We rested for about a half hour and when Bob's back was dry I re-saddled.

A HOT AFTERNOON

It was a slow, hot, four miles back to the Windmill Ranch now. We never hurry home, it's a bad habit for any horse. Makes them too anxious, spoiled and eventually awful hard to handle whenever traveling back home. Ever rode a rental horse home? When Brown Bob and I strolled into the Windmill corrals that late afternoon we acted as if it was just another days work. We were totally calm and rested by then. We never let on how much trouble and strain them dang bulls were. Everybody had a few sly questions about the "trip" and we parried them off with relaxed, confident, every day sort of answers.

Saying, "Nothin' to it boys, just another afternoon bit of ranchin' for me and ole Bob."

I became one of the "hands" now, for certain. That evening after a good supper at the married cowboy's electrified ranch house, I was introduced to the Bunkhouse almost a quarter mile from these other ranch buildings. The bunkhouse wasn't wired so we used oil lamps there. The boss, Duane and his wife, Beverly, had recently self constructed a new home up on the hilltop above the rest the ranch.

The bunkhouse was very old and in very poor condition. Needing much paint and repair to the weathered, clap-board construction. The screened door and windows had given up stopping pests. A thorough bug treatment was long overdue. It was overrun with spiders, scorpions, centipedes, wasps, hornets and other biting and stinging critters that were unnamed. One critter I only heard tell of was "The Walapai Tiger." I'm thinking it was an old-timers expression for the ten inch long yellow centipedes. Arizona scorpions are at least four inches long, with some much larger. Whatever it was, I wanted no part of its cruel hospitality. The lopsided outhouse out back was in the same shape. All we had for defense were a few cans of bug spray and a broom. In a few weeks we will be on the trail to the summer mountains. Sleeping out under the stars instead of cooped up with bugs. We all looked forward to that.

Nightly we slept with our clothes tucked into the folds of our bedrolls. We put one boot-top inside the other sos not to get a bad surprise in the morning. Strange critters would invade your boots overnight. Of course, we always vigorously shook everything out before we wore it each day. When we left in the early morning we almost never came back to this bunkhouse. Our days were spent working and all we did there at the bunkhouse was sleep... if we could.

A MEETING OF "MANES"

This first week at the Windmill Ranch, then called The DK Coconino Cattle Co., I spent gathering up my string of horses. Then shod them, late afternoons, after rounding up steers early every morning. The ranch always kept a large remuda of horses. They enjoyed their wild freedom most of the year. Only seeing us when they came near for water. We had to always track them down wherever they might freely roam. As years drifted by, the ranch stories told among us have all interwoven into one big roundup tale. Our discussions around campfires, dinner tables, bars, and old cow camps now make horses, dates, cowboys, and weather all come joyfully together as... "Remember that there one big roundup when..."

This following history will be just a fragment of an entire colorful stampede still galloping thru my memories. I plan to write very much more if the good Lord let's me live long enough.

DK SUMMER HEADQUARTERS

For a moment now let us think about the pleasant times we all have had around our fires.

I have had a fireplace just about all my life and lived outdoors with fires of all kinds. You might say I'm always easily enraptured when sitting by the flickering blaze of a campfire, fireplace or mesquite barbecue. Either with friends or all alone.

CAMPFIRES

Ever sit by a late evening campfire after a big steak dinner prepared over mesquite wood coals? If you haven't then let me tell you how that entraps you after everyone has retired and you are left there watching the last burning embers. Just tossing in a few little sticks to keep some light on your camp. Thinking, reminiscing, dreaming - - -

It's amazing how thoughts can so quickly switch from good memories to sad, disturbing ones. Then back again to loving memories of friends, loved ones, here and gone. Along with positive or negative decisions and too, too many dreams. Dreams you may have surely abandoned, others that you still may make come true...

A campfire has each it's own special individual magic. Large or small, roaring or smoldering, they tell their own message differently to each of us. Exciting stories are told and re-told by their side. Conversations about the twinkling stars above and loving memories are sweetly mellowed by a fires crackling warmth. Give yourself a campfire repose any chance you may get. It will always comfort your inner soul.

GATHER 'ROUND

It was a cold October
back in nineteen fifty four
Had a roundup camp for home
at a place called Casner Draw
Every evenin' ridin' back
and still feelin' sorta bold
After chasin' steers thru the pines
while dealin' with the cold

We all roped and drug in firewood
that lay along the trails
To heap upon the fires
where we recounted all our tales
You see it was the custom
to supply the cook with wood
But mere cowpokes couldn't use
the flames where the Cooky stood

We made our own blaze
about twenty foot away
There we punchers gathered every night,
each to have our say

Soon, by golly, all of us was a-laughin'
and a-jokein' up a storm
Can't say if it was the fire
or the stories that kept us warm

It started with the days gather
as we analyzed and ridiculed every word
Ira tracked a bunch for miles,
scooped them
up and drove 'em to the herd
Joe, he found that wild one
we'd all been watchin' for
Tied him to a gentle tree
and got his shirt all tore
Duane got into a pickle
when his pony bucked him down
But he never let go his reins
'cause he was a long,
long ways from town
This went on all thru the coffee,
biscuits, steak, and beans
More palaver past peach cobbler
and coffee as we squatted in our jeans
Each of us was, in turn,

reminded of a particular tale to tell
Then more coffee and some whiskey...
The fire captured us in its spell
We talked of mean horses
and gentle women
or 'twas it the other way around?
When we spoke of departed comrades...
There was no other sound

Just the cracklin' of the fire,
 the poppin' of pine knots
Breezes stirrin' thru the embers
while the cooky rattled pots
The night horse he's a-stompin'
with rollers in his nose
Could be a passin' bear
or hungry cougar I suppose

We're all gittin' sorta sleepy
just gazin' at them coals
A few bedrolls are unrolled
and we're huntin' up our holes
Some die-hard whiskey drinkers
are still are pitchin' in some sticks

To keep some light and warmth
thrown out upon this special mix

Most of us just listen now
as the older waddies reminisce
About cowboy life a long ways back
and the adventures we have missed
I find myself sorta dozin'
as I hunker in my roll
But I'm happy and content,
right on down to my cowboy soul!

CHAPTER FIFTEEN

Ranch Horses

I should tell you that when hiring on to a new ranch you must discuss what type of mounts were available. Especially if you are among the last one or two hands to arrive. It's best to avoid The *Rough String*, unless you are aiming at a Rodeo career. If you become among the last to get hired, the only mounts left to ride are the outlaws in the "rough string." Many horses are only ridden during the spring and fall roundups. Just a brief time with plenty of playful rest in between. The rough string are well bred, but nobody wants any of them on a regular basis. They all had acquired one or more bad habits over the years. Others are just plain mean or just liked to regularly buck and fight. They've had years of suffering the many mistakes made by inexperienced riders and just act like spoiled children. Most of them were turned out until a real bronc-buster showed up and wanted to try out his rodeo skills. Other times a man who was good with horses took some of them to re-train because he liked their looks and wanted the challenge. The rough string just sorta laid in wait ... until they might be desperately needed. Usually they were all that were left for *the last man hired.*

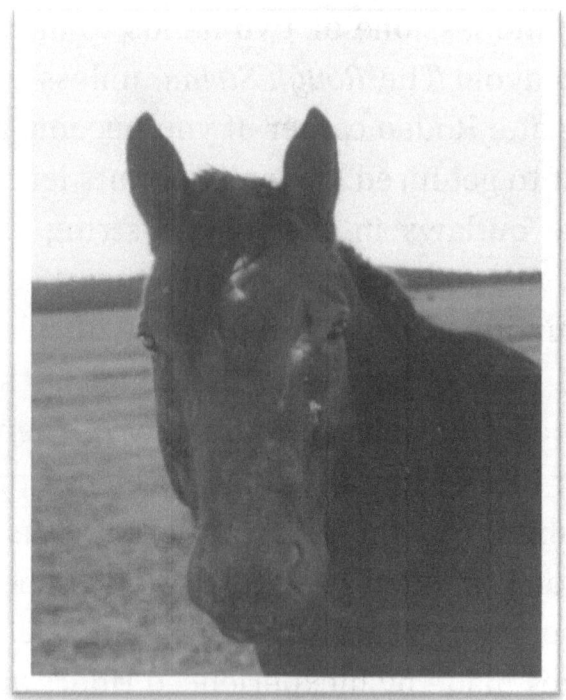

BLACK MARKET

UNRELATED TWINS

Let me deviate awhile to tell you a very unusual way we put the Rough String to work earning their keep. Please don't take our playful advice. I don't think this ever taught a horse a thing. But...It sure was fun back in the very early 50s, when we all were a little on the wild side!

With advanced planning, our part of Yavapai County would have an annual rodeo. Early spring was the best time. Before all the ranches rounded up and took their livestock up to the mountains new grass. Jointly we'd work together to supply all the labor and all the stock for our local show. Usually a three day, Friday, Saturday and Sunday party.

In those times it didn't take much more than a flank strap to make any animal buck. Riders and ropers were as available as Arizona sunshine and donated livestock were easy to haul in from nearby ranches. With a little pre-advertising we drew a fine crowd of stock, entrants and audience. Soon to fill the entries for all rodeo events for the three day show. Drawing many local cowboys and had even entrants of professional rodeo hands too, but mostly just statewide cowboy participants.

Here unfolds one of the many tales about how our Rough String performed and were also paid for their participation. Thus earning money for the DK Ranch.

We really didn't need the money but we wanted to haul a full ranch truck load of horses in to the fairgrounds. We brought our same bucking horses that were guaranteed to buck anywhere, anytime, plus to make a full truck we even brought some that just needed exercise. Added were these two, unrelated, twin-like horses. Mostly because the new hands that cut them out and ran them up the chute into the truck couldn't tell them apart ! They were just two black horses to them!

Off to the Rodeo went Black Market and Rooster. Only twins in appearance as they were both stocky built and black as ink. The only separating identifying mark was a small white spot hidden under Black Market's forelock.

That's the tuft of mane that hangs down the forehead between a horse's eyes. The horse who spent his time in our rough string was the all black horse called Rooster. Even kids could ride Back Market. However, usually, subjected to a "flank-strap" could make most any horse buck, jump and kick out to try to loosen it.

The first day when Rooster bucked out of the chute he unexpectedly made a terrific appearance. He lurched powerfully out the gate for about two jumps and immediately began a dizzying, bucking spin to the right. The rider got woozy after four or five whirls and never made the qualifying buzzer. In those older shows you must ride for ten seconds.

Two days later, we loaded Black Market into the saddle bronc chutes. Only we, who brought him there, knew it wasn't Rooster. Rodeo hands study all the bucking action every horse makes. They all buck differently. The riders want to know what they are in for so they can anticipate the bucking style and ride the mount they've drawn accordingly.

Of all the contestants to draw our inexperienced bucker, Black Market, it was the recent All-Indian, Fourth of July, Flagstaff Pow-Wow, saddle bronc champion! You could tell he was a champion by the way he confidently strutted up to the chutes. Darn! We now sorta pitied our Black Market kid horse. Shucks, it was his first show and the rider is going to scratch the horse with his spurs, from neck to flanks on both sides every jump!

That Navajo was about to crawl on the horse he *thought* was Rooster. Whom he watched bucking two days ago. Up the chute he climbed to make this boisterous bragging statement. Loudly shouting to everyone within hearing range he proclaimed, "I'm gonna ride this here crow-bait hoss clear back to Flagstaff, Arizona!"

That bold Navajo was ready for the supposed hard right-hand jump and spin that *Rooster* had made. Our duplicate horse knew nothing about rodeos and chutes. He only knew he must rid himself of that strap now in his very private flanks. The rider was ready.

Hunkering down. Even leaning slightly to the right to play right into that *probable* right hand whirl.

Well the ranch was twenty miles away and north to the *left,* when the Navajo's head-nod signaled for the chute gate to open! It was a fast explosion when the gate opened, releasing this large, muscular range horse Black Market. He wanted none of this stranger giving him un-kid like treatment that first jump.

Black Market was headed back home, *straight left!* Bucking close up along the line of bucking chutes, clearing a path through rodeo contestants and officials usually standing in the arena along the fence line. They scattered like quail under and over the fence. However, Mr. *"Champion of the Fourth of July, Pow-Wow"* was not aboard. He had only made the first jump but never saw that *left* turn the kid-horse made. He was on the ground right in front of the chutes. We picked up the dusty disillusioned rider, steadied him a bit and told him he was not even close to Flagstaff, Arizona.

Black Market had made it to the far end of the arena. I went down there and easily got ahold of him ... He had lost the flank strap and with his head over the fence he was gazing northward toward his ranch home miles away. A breeze crossed lightly past us and as the wind blew his forelock back, you could readily see that tell-tale spot under his forelock. That white dot seemed a mite brighter now! I think we both exchanged a smile.

A STRING OF MOUNTS

My first week at the DK was spent with my string of horses. Some were chosen for me and I even got to pick out a few myself, with the advice of the boss and the other cowhands. The older hand Cleve, gave me good advice. He became a kind, friendly saddle-pard. It was a long ago fifty-nine years but I think I had about ten head of horses. I'm hoping to remember their names and describe them correctly for you all. One for every day of the week and a few extra in case a horse got sick, or injured. We had a lot of hard riding to do and much work that must be accomplished. I had to keep them all healthy and shod. Most of the mounts we used were not real outlaws. Just a few with bad habits to be wary of.

BIMBO

In no particular order there was Bimbo, Jigger, Slim, Abdul, Janza, Cocomo, Mas Dulce, Pepper, Sam, Clabber, and Reno. Many others also rotated around in my string during all those years. After I became foreman I usually had first pick out of the remuda at the start of our roundups. First, after the boss, that is... When I was the year round hand, working mostly alone thru summers and winters I spent a lot of time training the outlaw horses to be better ranch horses. As I became older (and smarter) as foreman, I let the new hands try out the difficult horses. It was all only a game with us. Trying to "ride anything with hair on it," to show off our abilities just for the fun of it. The same challenge demonstrating our roping abilities, or...lack of same.

Clabber and Slim were the largest of my group. Both cream colored Palominos, their breeding went back to the Percheron stallion and thoroughbred mares the ranch had years ago. That was before Duane Miller, the son of Cecil Miller, the original owner, began introducing excellent Quarter horse stallions to these older mares. He took over the foreman/manager position for his father around 1950. Soon he was also replacing the old thoroughbred mares with well bred Quarter horses from sales all over the west and northwest. Duane grew up on this ranch with his brother, Cecil Jr. who later ran the 900 acre ranch farm down at Tolleson. They both learned the ranching and horse business from working side-by-side with many good cowboys.

HOW FAST AND HOW FAR

SLIM

Slim was a favorite dependable horse for everyone. If he wasn't such a giant of a slim Percheron the kids would have stolen him away from me. Children just had too much trouble getting on this very tall horse. The ranch kids already had two gentle horses to ride, Black Market and Tony. The old-timers respected him and would have wanted him in their string if he was only two or three hands shorter. I loved his friendly attitude and rode him a lot. It was a long way up to throw your saddle on him, but once saddled and mounted you were on a gentle warhorse.

He was brave and strong enough to drag anything around that your lariat would snare, but never use Slim to ride fence. It would wear you out climbing off and on this giant brute to fix fences all day. Slim never had a bad day with any rider. One advantage was you could see a cow a long ways off from way up there. He was so big and strong I was able to do a fun, show off trick to folks back then. I only weighed about 132 pounds and you may not believe this, but I could slide up his neck to ride, perched right behind his ears, with reins in hand, and boot heels back along his powerful neck. How's that for big and gentle?

CLABBER

Slim and Clabber had similar personalities once you got to know them, and they accepted you. Slim was totally willing at all times, but Clabber had to be reminded every day that he, too, was a good horse. He was more than just good because even as big as he was (over 1500 pounds) he was smooth to ride. Clabber was a pacer, a form of trotting, and he could pace all the day long.

A pacer moves by striding both legs forward and back, alternating, on each side when pacing. It is a comfortable ride without lots of jostling. An excellent horse to easily drive our big herd of horses many miles while making good time, too. It made the over forty-seven mile trip, from the mountain ranch to the lower valley ranch, almost a tolerable nine hours. We had the necessity to make this ride about a dozen times a year. Including the trips up and back with the stallion, and mare band twice a year. This was long before the pacing Paso Fino breed was even known in the west.

A South American breed that could pace all day, but they had too slight of a frame to do any hard work.

To ride Clabber without him trying and usually succeeding, in tossing you off numerous times each day, you had to start your day with him in a very assertive manner. If you didn't he would powerfully buck in a straight away style, gaining height and power with each successive jump. His more than three-quarter ton of range hardened form landing his stiff-legged forefeet in pain inflicting, jarring successions. Soon followed by you, flying high like a wounded buzzard, away from this torture. Coincidentally there were times when you also rode, reluctantly, behind his ears for a jump or two before the inevitable lift off!

To easily avoid this all you had to do, after saddling him up each day, was to jerk him around in circles both ways by his reins and cuss him out like you would to a man who stole your sweetheart, - - - then just brazenly climb aboard. He was yours from then on that day. You had to remember to re-introduce yourself, like that, each time you saddled him.

RENO

Reno, a red and white paint horse was ever so easy to sit upon, too. He had such a smooth gait that we said, "You have to get off every mile or just to let your bottom laugh."

He was not a pacer he was a single-footer. A single-footer trots along with his hind feet as the front feet lope. Reno could almost do this all day long. There was a price to pay to get this comfy ride, tho... This sweet horse had a dirty, nasty habit of being an awful kicker while being shod! You could easily shoe the front two hooves, but dare not touch any hair below the hocks of the hind legs. He would kick out straight back, like lightning, if you so much as tickled a hair on either lower hind leg.

The other cowhands said, with sinister smiles, "I could have him and his easy ride,... If I could shoe him."

There are harsh ways to shoe a horse like this. Involving tying him down on the ground, trussing up all four of his legs and wrestling the shoes on that-a-way. He was a friendly, quiet horse in most other situations so I didn't care to put him thru this trauma. Soon I thought of a way to get him shod. I'd shoe him by only holding onto his hooves.

Little by little, after days of shoeing his front feet, while touching, regularly, only his hind hoofs, I became a familiar pest. I also spoiled him with hand fed oats during those same lessons. Picking up a hoof by only the hoof, then became a careful but easy job. If you call easy that odd way of hanging on.

When he became very acceptable to all this I started to place the bent hoof on my knee. That gave us both a time of rest in that position. If I accidentally touched some hair growth close to the hoof he flinched and sometimes pulled away. Time and patience was the key to success. Reno began to like the daily attention I gave him, and the quiet, full attention we gave each other.

This is an uncomfortable way to do the shoeing steps. He was fine in that half- cocked position resting easily on my knee. I had to rest often, but it was only two hooves to measure and shape, only two to trim and level. Usually, six nails in a shoe were enough to hold a shoe on for eight weeks or maybe nine in the dryness of Arizona weather. Two more nails could go in the front forward two holes of the shoe. I always put the two extra nails in! You don't want to lose a shoe, when they are so tedious to replace.

I then became the envy of all my saddle-pards. Riding along so fancy and handsomely on this much desired, gentle, easy traveling, "Single-Footer." I still see Reno every evening above our fireplace in a photo among his remuda of cow-horse compadres. Standing beautifully alert in his spotted red and white paint horse coat. It makes me smile to see him again every night and still... "It makes other parts of me laugh!"

MAS DULCE

A few years on, when we got smarter, we sometimes used a tranquilizer on tough to shoe horses. Did I mention that we also were doing most all our own Veterinary work, too. Being far from town you couldn't always call a Vet. Hell, we didn't even have a telephone all those years. Most animal medicines were easy to buy in those days so we bought some tranquilizer, some penicillin, dyhrodostrepto - - -somthin' etc, etc.,... But Mas Dulce, meaning *more sugar* in Spanish, was another problem, but good, horse in my string. He was tough to shoe, altho he didn't kick. But, my! oh! my! He sure could struggle and fight the procedure.

All the hands helped me shoe him by laying him down many times. All tied up like a captured calf at a rodeo, still struggling. After giving him a shot of the medicine it was then easy to casually throw on a set of shoes while he stood calmly. We sure worked a lot of cattle together...Until, the mistake.

The mistake being we didn't know anything about anaphylactic shock. During one shoeing, he began waking up to soon. I was midway with the last shoe as the struggling began.

I'll just give him a few more CCs of the tranquilizer so I can finish, I thought. That additional repeat shot put him into shock. Something we did not even know about then. Sadly, had we kept some epinephrine around we could have brought him out of that. In thirty minutes he died. Afterwards we stocked that antidote.

JIGGER

I spent lots of time aboard my favorite mount, Jigger. He was tough as nails, and never gave up on a steep mountain climb, a steer chase, or a long boring days ride fixing fence. Jigger feared no trail, or rock strewn passage. He was game to climb up or down anything and crash through any thorny cactus or bush. His always shiny dark brownish black hide was part

Thoroughbred and part Morgan. He represented both breeds majestically.

SYCAMORE CANYON COUNTRY

Sometimes he showed his nervous side, but always kept in full control of the task at hand. Jigger and I encountered bears in the wild on different occasions. He never flinched or backed down even after getting a good whiff of their strong scent. His worst display of nervousness was only about every morning when you first mounted up. Jigger was always poised to whirl away to the right when you lifted on and swung across the saddle. Most horses are taught to move to the left, under you, or stand still as you mount.

I, in turn, stayed always ready by having a left hand full of mane and a very short, tucked in right rein. Still he always did managed to twist away partially to the right and spin as best he could. When I soon caught up with my right stirrup he knew I was set tight and could calm down his gyrations. I'd have to loosen up then on his reins, too. Then, sometimes, he would make a few attempts at bucking me off. I didn't mind because we both knew I could easily pull his head up to reel him in. These were only his playful, happy to be alive, jumps and so our days began. He only did that first thing in the morning. Being all gentleman the rest of the day.

PEPPER

When I first arrived at the DK, Pepper was in Harry Davis' string. A nicely built, well muscled, dappled grey thoroughbred type. His long black mane and tail always flying in the wind as he tried to buck Harry off every morning. Pepper never got any bad treatment from Harry for his pitchin'. Harry liked riding him because he could then practice his rodeo riding techniques. Pepper put on a morning show, then for the rest of the day he was all cow-horse.

He was so doggone pretty I always wanted him in my string. When I rode with Harry I always watch his morning style as well as Peppers and thought I could ride like that too. When Harry went on to rodeos and other ranches I quickly gathered Pepper up into my string. Of course I couldn't ride as good as Harry but I had a gentle way of treating a horse. After a week or two of attempting to lose me Pepper just quieted down and we became friends. He'd playfully crow-hop around sometimes but never got in earnest to buck me off anymore. I rode Pepper often because he was easy to shoe, travelled smoothly at any gait, and was such a good lookin' grey horse. He, too, is in Joe Beelers painting, Nature Of A Cowhorse, along with Sam and Preacher.

COCOMO

Can't brag about Cocomo much since we just didn't fit together. Fit is a good operative word. He and I sure did not get along well. All thru the training procedure from halter breaking, saddling, getting accustomed to the bit, and reining, he was a little terror. Cocomo objected to everything except the grooming. He loved to be brushed and have the tangles taken out of his mane and tail. He was a dandy of a lithe, wiry, agile, red sorrel horse. He wanted to look as pretty as he really was. Even enjoyed being properly shod without protest.

But Lord, he hated to be tacked up and fought it all the time. His first thirty days of our initial acquaintance I had to hobble all four feet to begin our daily afternoon training sessions. To protect his legs and ankles I made hobbles with the burlap sacks our oats came in then. Once opened up completely they became a square burlap sheet. This sheet I rolled up diagonally making a long soft smooth snake. With about four hemp tie strings it became secured in that shape. It was much softer and thicker than a rope would be on his ankles. I used one *snake* for his forefeet and another for the hind legs. His early lessons were mostly with all four feet tied and the forward and back hobbles then tied together at their center. The soft cotton rope tie between was left about four foot long. In this set-up, ornery Cocomo could not lunge very far.

I spent many months working with this horse but he never gave up trying to buck me off. Yes, he became three years old and finally liked his ranch work once he got warmed up, but he wasn't ever like my other students. Those, I eventually, could trust. It is very tiresome having to closely watch your mounts temperament all day so when he became four years old I let another hand try him out. Ellsworth Varagee was a good puncher so when he began I warned him about this horses style. Ellsworth was not a rough-string rider. He had ridden with me often when I was on Cocomo and knew this horse's habits. Making matters worse he also wore Bat-wing chaps. Shot-gun chaps are like leather pants put on over your Levis. Bat-wing chaps are the wild, flappy kind you see on bucking horse rodeo riders. They are easy to make and were first on the southwest ranges. On ranches today they have become an old style. Shot-guns give more protection from the brush, thorns, rain, and cold.

In Cocomo's life and mine, Bat-wings were a threat to us both. I then also wore Bat-wing chaps. When a strong wind came up behind us it would sometimes blow one or both of these hanging flappy ears up near Cocomo's shoulders. A surprise he never expected or tolerated without trying to buck!

In the 50s and 60's many cowhands still liked these Bat-wings. Ellsworth had a set of these, too. They were sure to flip-flap in the air on occasions. If there was something urgent to attend to and you spurred your horse up into a quick gallop while charging after a loose cow, those ears would charge up and down too. A flipping and flopping that seemed like elephant ears behind any horse. Ellsworth's first day aboard Cocomo arrived and we all anticipated the inevitable wreck. Our morning ride began by giving all the advice and cautions we could muster. Ellsworth was just too relaxed we thought. The first thirty minutes were calm as we five rode up to a forked trail-head. We pulled our mounts to a halt as the Boss gave us each our search and gather locations. Mentioning where to all meet up, later, with our rounded up steers.

Ellsworth was told to follow the long draw ahead, we others slowly went our own directions. We left slowly so we could watch Ellsworth's parting progress. I was personally concerned because I *did not* want to see a bronc ride. But how could it not happen since this horse was, forever, trying me out daily? Well, Ellsworth lit out in a fast trot and then broke into a long lope.

Bat-wings soon bouncing up and fluttering madly. To the surprise of us all, Cocomo paid no heed to this. He worked like the cow-horse I always wanted him to be. From that day, he never bucked again. We never knew how this magical change came over him. I always treated him kindly because I liked that little horse, but could not settle him down. He certainly liked Ellsworth and they became partners the entire roundup. Something changed that horse that day and for the rest of his life he never pitched again. What caused this turn around we would never understand. It's another strange occurrence that comes about in the lives and minds of horses. Cocomo evolved into a safe horse for all his following riders. Often, I stroked his head while telling him how proud he made me and his other riders, but I never rode him again. I sadly recollect, he was one of the very few horses that disliked me.

SAM

Sam, a Strawberry Roan. Roans are different shades of color. Our ranch had a Red Roan Stallion, Redwood Jake, for eighteen years. Sired by Redman, he was mostly a pastel type grayish body covered completely with small spots and hues of reddish colors. Grey, or white horses have black woven in to make them somewhat Roanish. Others have a blue color mixed in to make a Steel Blue Roan." Only horses like Sam are colored like the legend, the poem and a song. "The Strawberry Roan."

BOB GARVEY RIDIN' A STRAWBERRY ROAN

Sam was too nice to be as wild as that legend goes. He was fast and furious in everything he did, but if you could ride, then together, you could do any cowboy job. Just before I retired the ranch gave Sam to one of our retirees. He was living on his old homestead, in a now overcrowded town, but had a place to keep a horse. We gave him Sam because he had rode him years ago and liked him a lot. Sam was not safe for children, but he was like a rocking chair to an experienced old cowboy. Ira was almost eighty then and Sam had gotten old too. Old in years, not in their minds.

I watched Red make a great cow-horse out of Bimbo. We all agreed that every great horse has a flaw somewhere. The perfect horse still lives only in our future training plans. None of us had the ability to correct Bimbo's one drawback. His powerful, chunky conformation with very short pasterns, made him a rough riding S.O.B. You did not have an easy ride at any of Bimbos gaits. Walking was bearable, but you hardly made any progress at all with his short steps. Trotting was sheer torture to your spine and cheeks, while loping was a bearable jerking motion. Did he ever smooth out? Only when you opened him up full bore, at a dead run, was he the horse you wanted in your string. He would speed you anywhere and never tire. However you can't do this all day. But when after a getaway steer it was a good bet he could catch, or outrun, any cow on any terrain invented by the devil himself! There was no getting this horse away from Red. After a few years Red got a wife. Next they got citified and Red quit and lit out for the big town of Phoenix. It wasn't long until those palomino full brothers, Abdul and Bimbo, were both in my string.

It was true, Bimbo was the roughest riding, excellent horse, I ever rode. I chose the times to ride him very carefully. Only on short circles, cutting cattle, rocky slow traveling and most of all, on the days you really needed a wild cow catching horse. When Bimbo had a wild steer on the end of your rope, he sure knew how to handle him. He was a swift, nimble footed, cutting horse that could dodge the hooking and butting of any angry steer. He could have been a bulldogging horse. He just loved to get in close to a running animal. Many times after losing my lariat to a runaway roped steer he would take me right up to the head of that steer so I could lean over, and pick up my lost lasso. I learned a spectacular trick for chasing a loose rope from a ranch savvy Mexican vaquero one fall. He had the misfortune to catch a large strong wild steer and lost his dallies almost immediately. I was following close at his heels on Bimbo to give assistance. He never lost sight of that steer and pursued him coolly, while making his horse step on the trailing lasso. When all went as he planned his horse stepped on the rope and it pulled taunt as it sizzled under the shod hoof. When it popped loose, up into the air in a high arc, he spurred quickly up into that arc, catching the flying, elusive twine.

His real problem was his saddle-horn. It was not wrapped round and round like ours with old cotton rope, or used inner tube rubber. It wasn't even a fat-necked dally-horn. So he again lost his slippery dallies and the steer. I sped past him, Bimbo leaning in close and fast, to the steer's head. I leaned over, grasped the line at the steers neck and turned off, putting on about three dally-wraps to stop the steer.

This vaquero, named Chavez, was so determined, embarrassed and angry (at himself), he begged me to let him lead this last steer into the nearby shipping corrals. He felt it was his duty to succeed. I handed him his retrieved rope and off he happily went again. The steer, now really wild, upset, and blowing snot, was still much on the fight. It wasn't long until the skinny slick saddle-horn was, again, Chavez's undoing.

The steer broke free, slobbering wildly as he breezed swiftly past the shipping pens, the transport trucks and wide-eyed drivers. Then jumped the last holding fence to freedom. Bimbo and I arrived at the fence as the rope was sliding over the top wire. Again Bimbo put me in position to lean over and snag the loose rope before all of it and the steer were gone. Quickly taking my wraps, the chase came to its end.

Our entire crew had been trying to capture this steer for over two weeks and we were all so glad to have him now weighed and loaded on the truck. He was a remnant from last year's roundup, and had escaped many times.

He and two others had even survived the brutal Flagstaff winter. Now over two years old he should have been 1200 pounds, but our many unsuccessful chases had him in marathon shape. He weighed only about 950 pounds. He'd been teaching other young steers all the getaway tricks. Causing them to be as hard to handle as he was. He became "cowboy public enemy number one" for over a year now. Needless to say we were happy to ship him away to the California feed lots.

GEORGE ON ABDUL

ABDUL

I surely didn't make this list in order of my favorites. It's too hard to choose, anyway. I shall always remember Abdul. A Palomino Paint horse. I reckon there ain't many of them because the color scheme is so unusual. Palominos have basic colors. Beautiful colors of gold, tan, crème, etc., etc.. Then the paint color comes from a different parent of just about any color. It is not guaranteed, but sometimes splashed on in spots over the horse to make an outstanding unusual color-combo.

Abdul was a year younger than his full brother Bimbo. Same stallion, same dam, but although they were both Palominos only Abdul was palomino paint. Bimbo was a complete palomino cream color from head to hoof. Abdul grew up and in a year he had palomino tannish-cream spots over parts of his white frame. Seems that Bimbo took after his Pa, and Abdul favored his Ma. Bimbo was a short coupled Quarter horse type, and Abdul was more streamlined like his thoroughbred Dam.

Each year we started many ranch horses. We divided up the foals between the winter hands for their first lessons with cowboys. You had the right to name the horse you were training. That fall a good puncher named Red took on this horse he named Bimbo. Gave him his first 30-40 days initial training and turned him back out until spring roundup. The following additional spring training and riding made him a very sought after all round cow horse

The following fall I picked Bimbo's twin brother to train. Since they were so identical in family I turned that horses name into the reverse of Bimbo. This came out as Obmib. That didn't last long. Obmib looked like a steed out of the Arabian Nights and his name gravitated around to Abdul Obmib. Very much sounding like a romantic horse of the Arabian desert. The name Abdul fitted him from then on.

He helped transform his Quarterhorse blood by both his appearance and attitude. A striking palomino paint with his white body spotted with different patterns of palomino tan made him unlike his full brother Bimbo. Abdul was sleek, long and tall while Bimbo was a powerful, short-coupled muscular Quarter type. We made quite a wild picture when charging thru the trees after a fleeing bunch of steers. His long mane flashing in the sun as his eagle eyes and lithe body pursued the cattle. There was no territory too rugged for him or Bimbo. Full speed was their only gear when asked to chase. Straight up or down, rocky, smooth, or muddy, they never halted. Stumbling, but always recovering, never going down. Thorny cactus and brush never tuned them when on the chase. They both loved their ranch work as we did.

One day, after the steers we were after were halted and settled down, I noticed blood on the rocks around me. Dismounting, I quickly examined my horses legs. Abdul had never flinched, or limped but there was a deep gash in his right fore-foot that went clear around to a long split in his hoof.

The shoe was gone, and the gash on the inside of one of his heels was very large. We were in serious trouble. Without attention the entire bulb of his outside heel and a large part of his hoof would soon tear off. We were three miles from camp. My saddle-pard sadly exclaimed he was crippled for life!

I was wearing a shirt and Levi jacket. I took off my shirt and with my pocket knife I fashioned a few bandages and ties out of it. Even a soft patch for the worst bleeding at the rear of this injury. Abdul was very patient and understanding. He knew I would do my very best. There seemed to be no pain because his adrenalin was still flowing. If we could make it to the camp where our horse trailer was I could haul him the eighteen miles back to the main ranch. There we had a better medicine chest.

Working feverishly I fashioned a pretty good temporary combo shoe and bandage to that hoof. It had a large bulbous appearance and wasn't much on looks, but the blood had begun to coagulate and the numerous knotted bandage ties I made seemed to hold it all together. The other cowhand got the steers on the trail and I slowly followed behind.

The steers were over their fear of us and settled down to a slow walk to water at our camp. After a bit we were on a good forest road with easy traveling. Abdul was oblivious to his injury. Occasionally my pard had to quickly go to the lead and slow down a few steers that wanted to hurry away as we quietly and carefully kept them in a good frame of mind. Abdul bravely made his way with only a slight limp. He always knew the way back to his hay dinner. I was sad and worried, but determined to make him recover.

We arrived in time to put the steers in with other cattle we had gathered and left quickly with our horses loaded in the trailer. I spent the evening cleaning, disinfecting, doctoring and bandaging that hoof with good supplies from the first aide collection of our barn's horse hospital supplies.

This became a twice a day ritual for 2 weeks, then only once a day for months. It was almost a year later that we decided the hoof and heel were sound enough for me to ride Abdul again. Being doubly sure, I could also see by his daily frisky attitude, that he thought that way too. Always, I thanked the Lord for giving him back to me.

Here is a picture of my TONY who lives with me today.

He is now twenty years old and my last horse. Tony, a palomino, that will always remind me of my palomino paint, Abdul.

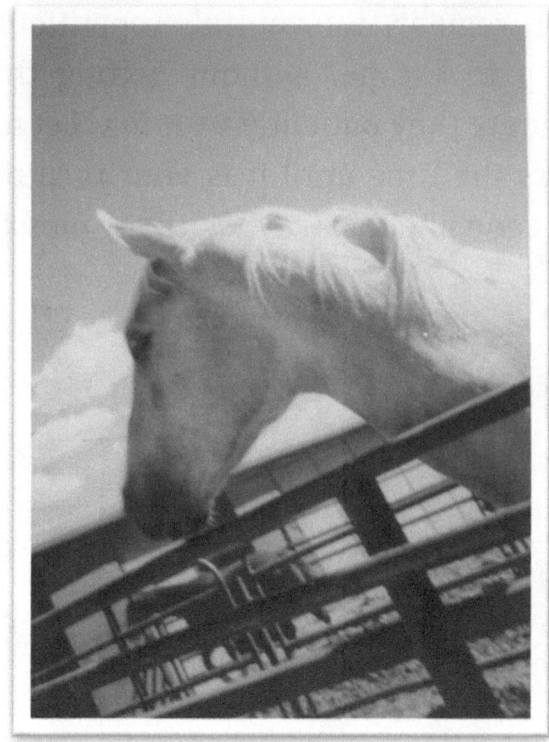

TONY

You can now understand how a ranch remuda of almost 100 horses can stir up a lifetime of interesting stories I've written many other stories about my ranching adventures with all of them. If this is interesting to you please watch for my next few books. I'd like you all to enjoy these adventures with me.

Many adventurous people have been for years, or what have seemed like years, chained to their regular, uneventful, repetitious jobs. Yearning to escape, without getting that one opportunity they patiently wait for. Let me help you pass the time until it is your turn to leave your cocoon and fly away...With my blessings.

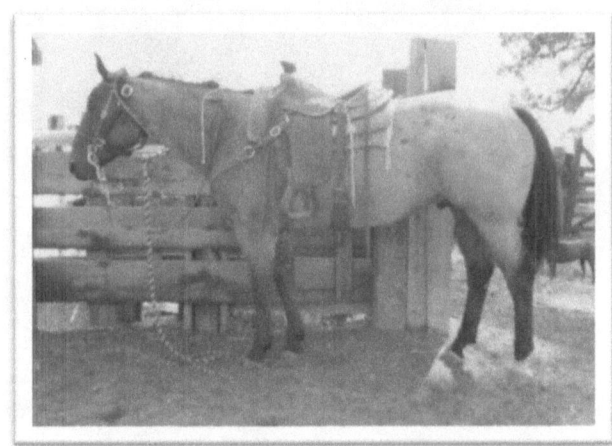

JANZA

CHAPTER SIXTEEN

The Star Brand

Cowhands think they'll continue to avoid the grim reaper no matter what they may encounter. Wild broncos, wild cattle, along with a bull or two, or falling off a windmill are regular hazards that go along with the trails they follow. Other times, treacherous trails along a high steep canyon could *maybe* be the end. But they rely on the *"maybe"*, thinking they will always survive.

It's the following weeks of pain we only dread. Working, while still hurting from an accident, is the only fearful time we are constantly trying to avoid. If they ever presumed they would go to heaven after havin' a hell-of-a-life down here, I'm sure it will be the Heaven, I'm personally aiming at in this rhyme.

THE STAR BRAND

I once had a dream boys,
so real it must be true
'bout the cowboy's place in heaven
when God's roundup is thru
Seems like my top-hoss
and me where at the ole Pearly Gates
Along with lots of other folks,
one and all just waitin' our fate

Then the great tally was taken
and the good Lord called my name

I asked, "Are there cows in Heaven,
Cowboyin' is why I came
His laughter thundered 'or the sky
and he said "Son, come along"
I'll show you our cowboy Heaven
where nothin' ever goes wrong

Well boys, it was amazin',
them sights just left me numb
I'll tell you what I remember then
 we'll all know what's to come
First thing I noticed was the range,
just as green as it could be
Stretchin' out across the Heavens
as far as I could see

No water-tanks are needed here,
there's a spring every mile or so
Supplied with a natural salt-lick,
just as pure and white as snow
This country can't be overgrazed,
there's grass for stock and game
Who live contented all the time,
which makes 'em very tame

There're never bothered by the flies,
ain't ever a one been sick
They don't get struck by lightning bolts,
or hurt so much as a nick
Each one is branded with a STAR,
that includes the horses too
Clear nights you can make a tally,
but it's quite a chore to do

There's even a pasture set aside for ponies
that's had their day
And when yore old horse leaves ya,
he's out in that Milky Way
Just agrazin' and awaitin'
for that day to come around
When you'll be there to greet him...
on that sacred ground

The Headquarters is just as modern
as any cowhand ever knew
With every little this and that
to make a happy crew
But the line-camps are old fashioned

to supply some atmosphere
'Cause a sure-nuff puncher "roughs it"
thru parts of every year

Up there the cook ain't grumpy
and the chuck tastes pretty good
Why he even says a "Thank-Ya"
when you drag up a little wood
All the ponies savvy cow work,
each one a real top-hoss
With none of them bad habits
that make a cowpoke cross

The killers and the mean outlaws
must range the devil's lair
While rodeo buckers like ole Midnight
still pitch at shows up there
The ropers got all their fingers
and they never miss a throw
Which eliminates the cussin'...
That ain't allowed ya know!

Yore never caught out in a storm
minus a slicker and dry match

And that slicker got all its buttons
with nary a hole or patch
Prairie dog and badger holes
are all set well aside
And your ole horse never stumbles
no matter where you ride

There ain't no wire, ain't no fence,
ain't no traps around the waters
Just pole corrals and chutes
that's really needed at Headquarters
You get the best of wages,
that's including' room and board,
But it's not cash or checks ya get
when yore workin' for the Lord

The payroll is chock-full of things
that money could never buy
Tho some folks will never see their value,
no matter how they try
There's wind to cool the air
when the sun is blazin' down
Rain that makes the grass grow tall,
gives the crew a day in town

The sun pays off his chore of makin'
each day warm and bright
The moon lights the Night-Hawks
way circlin' the remuda at nite
There's the beauty and the color
placed all around us by His Hand
That is surely a great blessing
that only later we'll understand

Yes I said this was a dream
but I reckon I made a slip
"I knew you'd finally notice
the STAR branded on my ponies hip
So, adios for now boys,
I'll see you again... Someday
After this worldly cowhands life
has left you weary and grey

I'll be leadin' an extra horse that day
and I wouldn't ride' that far
Unless, that extra bronc is yours
and he's branded with a STAR !

ADIOS UNTIL NEXT TIME!
THE LAST DK COWBOY

Stay in Touch with George!
lastdkslashcowboy@gmail.com

Be Sure to Visit His Website:
www.lastdkcowboy.com

www.ingramcontent.com/pod-product-compliance
Lightning Source LLC
Chambersburg PA
CBHW021044130626
46552CB00005B/2003